Small Mercies

BY BRIDGET KRONE

Catalyst Press
Pacifica, California

In North America, this book is distributed by
Consortium Book Sales & Distribution, a division of Ingram.
Phone: 612/746-2600
cbsdinfo@ingramcontent.com
www.cbsd.com

Small Mercies is published by Catalyst Press.

In the UK and Commonwealth, *Small Mercies*
is published by Walker Books.

For rights information, please contact
Catalyst at info@catalystpress.org.

FIRST EDITION
10 9 8 7 6 5 4 3 2 1

Library of Congress Control Number: 2019954217

For Davie and Simon

AFRICA

ATLANTIC
OCEAN

INDIAN
OCEAN

SOUTH
AFRICA

PIETERMARITZBURG

In South Africa, the word "coloured" is used to describe mixed-race people whose descendents are a combination of Asian (Malay or Indian), black, white, and/ or Khoisan. Coloured people, especially those that live in the Western Cape, speak mainly Afrikaans, but about 20% have English as their home language. Many are bi-lingual or speak other African languages as well.

In America the term "coloured" is considered offensive but in South Africa its use is widespread and more acceptable, if sometimes controversial. The discussion about race and identity is on-going: some people reject the term "mixed race" as it suggests that they don't have a distinct race, and claim the term "coloured" with pride, while others identify themselves as black, Khoisan, or just "South African."

Though we spell "color" in this book the American way, we have kept the British spelling "coloured" to refer to this particular cultural group of South Africa to distinguish it from the American usage of the term, which has a different history.

CHAPTER 1

Mercy stood in front of the principal's desk, with the excuse note in her hand. Mrs. Griesel laid down her pen and looked at her over the top of her spectacles.

"Yes, Mercy?" she said, taking the note and opening it. "It says here that you are to be excused from the class assembly rehearsals because you have..." She paused and looked at Mercy as if she couldn't quite believe what she was reading. "The *collywobbles*?"

Mercy nodded.

"Are the collywobbles the same or different from the dickey tummy you had last week?" Mrs. Griesel heaved herself out of her swivel chair and clip clopped over to a filing cabinet from which she pulled a file.

"I must have about twelve excuse notes here," she said. "This one was rather good. It says that you are to be excused from inter-house cross-country because you have a bone in your leg." She raised one eyebrow. "Who wrote this note, Mercy?"

"My foster mother, Aunt Mary."

"Did she also write the one about you having a bone in your leg?"

"No, that was my other foster mother, Aunt Flora."

"Yes, I remember now. They're sisters."

Mrs. Griesel tapped her top lip with her index finger. "And, just remind me, how long have you been living with these aunts?"

"Since I was five."

"And they are...how old would you say?"

Mercy didn't know. When she'd asked Aunt Mary a few years ago, Aunt Mary said she was as old as her tongue and a little bit older than her teeth. They were old—but it was hard to say just how old. Their faces were lined and freckled and their hair was silvery white: Aunt Mary cut hers straight with nail scissors but Aunt Flora's hair stood up like dandelion fluff. Aunt Mary always carried a handkerchief and a bunch of keys in the pocket of her homemade dress. Aunt Flora liked comfy tracksuit pants that she pulled up high. How old is that exactly?

"I don't know, Mrs. Griesel."

"So why has Mrs. Pruitt sent you to me today? Tell me more about this class assembly and why you need to be excused from it."

It was hard for Mercy to explain why the instruction to do a folk dance from her own culture proved so difficult to follow. When she asked the aunts for help, they didn't make it any easier.

"Oh for heaven's sake," Aunt Mary said, when Mercy asked. "Can we pretend you are Polish and teach you the polka?"

Aunt Mary had ideas about education and they didn't include cultural folk dancing or anything "new-fangled" as she called it. She didn't even read Mercy's school reports. She thought education should include memorizing the

Latin names of plants and a lot of great poetry. *Oh young Lochinvar has come out of the West, through all the wide border his steed was the best...*

But Aunt Flora was more nervous: she liked Mercy to get the right answer and not get into trouble.

"What should we do, Mary?" Aunt Flora said. "Shall we teach her the quick step?"

But they decided in the end to teach her Morris dancing.

So Mercy watched while Aunt Flora played a plinky-plonky tune on the piano and Aunt Mary skipped about the sitting room waving her handkerchief in time to the music. Aunt Mary was not a person who skipped lightly and Mercy had been a bit disturbed by the sight—and then relieved when Aunt Mary had come to a breathless halt saying, "Oh, this is ridiculous. We'll have to think of something else."

After an awkward silence, Aunt Flora asked, "Well, what will the other children be doing?"

"Indian dancing? Maybe Zulu dancing," Mercy offered. "Mrs. Pruitt said that we all have a culture and we must celebrate it."

"Ridiculous," said Aunt Mary. "Almost no one has a single culture. If I were in your class at school, Mercy, which culture would I celebrate? White South African, whatever that is? Viking? English? West Indian?"

"West Indian?" Mercy was confused.

"Yes. After our great grandmother died, my great grand-father married a West Indian woman and it's one of the big regrets of my life that I've never gone to Barbados to meet that side of my family."

"Mrs. Pruitt wants me to do something by these people called the Cape Malay Minstrels," said Mercy. "Maybe it's because I'm...you know...coloured."

"Just because your mother's people came from Cape Town originally is no reason, dear child, to go capering about in shiny satin twanging a small guitar. Honestly! If you had grown up on the Cape Flats, it would be a festival that you could take completely to heart, but you've never even *been* to Cape Town!"

Mercy was relieved. She'd seen the Kaapse Klopse festivities on TV; seen the bright costumes, the brass bands and the colorful umbrellas, but the whole event was completely alien to her; it was as strange as a Chinese New Year street party with paper dragons.

"So," said Aunt Mary, "If we are to be accurate, I think what we are looking for here is a dance that has some Cape Malay, some Khoisan, a bit of Dutch Settler, some English..."

"I think we'll just write a little excuse note, shall we?" Aunt Flora said, always anxious to get Aunt Mary off her high horse. "Now where did I put those..." And she wandered off through the kitchen and out into the back garden, patting her pockets and the top of her head, looking for her spectacles.

So it was Aunt Mary who found a pen and wrote the note about the collywobbles—the same note that Mrs. Griesel was now adding to Mercy's folder as she waited for an explanation.

Mercy took a deep breath. "Our class is in charge of assembly on Friday and Mrs. Pruitt wants us to do folk dancing from our own culture."

"What a good idea!" said Mrs. Griesel, beaming. "I don't understand why your aunts would want you to miss out on this very worthwhile cultural activity. It sounds like such fun. Don't you agree, Mercy?"

"Yes ma'am."

Mrs. Griesel made her hands into a church steeple to support her chin and looked at Mercy with narrowed eyes.

"I have to confess, you're a bit of a mystery, Mercy Adams," she said, looking back down at the folder. "Your marks are excellent but you won't join in. You won't do sport at all. Or orals. Or plays. You want to be excused from *everything*." Mrs. Griesel sighed. "And the peculiar thing is that these foster mothers of yours seem to collude in this non-participation. They seem to encourage it."

She changed her tone of voice and tilted her head at a caring angle. "Mercy, is everything all right at home?"

"Yes. It's all fine," said Mercy quickly. "Everything's fine."

Mrs. Griesel looked back down at the open folder, flapped some pages backwards and forwards, and asked a bit too casually, "When did the social worker last check on you?"

Mercy dug her fingernails into the palm of her hand.

"I think I need to contact Child Welfare to review your case." Mrs. Griesel made a note in her diary. "I'm sure it's time they extended the order." She paused and then she said under her breath: "It may be time to reconsider..."

"It's OK, Mrs. Griesel, ma'am," Mercy said as brightly as she could. "I'll do the dancing."

"That's the spirit, Mercy," said Mrs. Griesel, leaning back in her chair. "A little dancing will do you so much good." She wrinkled her nose. "You might even enjoy it."

Mercy was prepared to do almost anything, even skip around waving a white hanky in the air, if it would keep the social worker away from the house.

CHAPTER 2

Not long ago, Aunt Mary told Mercy that she was old enough to understand the problem with social workers.

"If we wanted to get a dog from the SPCA," she said, "someone would come to our house beforehand to check that we have a garden big enough for the dog to run about and bark, and a proper fence so that it couldn't run away and get lost."

Mercy nodded, thinking a bit sadly that even the smallest dog would be able to hop over the low wall that surrounded their house in Hodson Road.

"But if someone wants to foster a *person*, a child, like you," said Aunt Mary, "I just fill out a paper called a Form 36 at the Department of Social Development; then I can take you home and get the grant each month from SASSA. There's a social worker who is supposed to do a 'home circumstances visit,' but she might have about two hundred children on her files. So she probably won't ever come to check if we have a fence or if our garden is big enough for running about in. Or barking."

"But sometimes," Aunt Mary continued, holding both of Mercy's hands tightly, "the social workers do come. It's usually on a Friday afternoon—just as the courts are about to close for the weekend, and they wave a piece of paper called 'a court order.' They might say that there is a relative who has come forward and wants to take you."

"And then what happens?"

"Well, they can take you away."

"Away! Why would they do that?"

"For money, I'm sorry to say," Aunt Mary said. "They arrange with a so-called family that they will get the grant from SASSA and the social worker gets a cut."

This information filled Mercy with dread. Would her Uncle Clifford come and find her?

"But the reason I'm telling you is that there is something we can do if that happens," Aunt Mary said. "I've tried teaching Flora the words—in case I'm not at home and a social worker pitches up at the door. But she gets in such a muddle these days, so you need to learn these words off by heart as well."

She handed Mercy a paper on which was written:

"According to the Children's Act of 2010, each child has the right to legal representation and I demand that the order be held pending this process."

"This means that you are allowed to get a lawyer to help you before *they* can take you away. It's the law, though some people don't know this."

Mercy had the words engraved on her heart. And she repeated them to herself every day—like a lucky charm to ward off evil.

CHAPTER 3

On her way from Mrs. Griesel's office to her classroom, Mercy stopped at the bathroom. She stared at her face in the mirror and took a deep breath to calm the beating of her heart. Her face was changing into someone she hardly knew: her nose was growing like a mushroom; her teeth had become so big and long and, where previously she'd had soft cheeks, she now had bony angles. Only her brown eyes remained the same.

"Oh you've got a lovely face," Aunt Flora said when she saw Mercy sticking a tongue out at herself in the bathroom mirror. She cupped Mercy's chin in her hand. "Just like your beautiful mother and your Aunty Kathleen." But Mercy felt she no longer recognized this angular new face of hers.

She smoothed her hair with both hands to settle the curls that would not lie flat and pulled her small ponytail tight.

Back in the classroom, everyone was moving desks out of the way to make space for the cultural dancing. She hoped no one would notice her slip to the back of the room.

Mrs. Pruitt was standing by the blackboard looking tense and thin; the extension cable was too short to reach the portable CD player and she was standing holding the machine in mid-air, looking for someone to help her.

"Someone shove that desk closer," she said. "I am not a shelf."

It was the new girl Olive who helped and she pushed the desk so hard, it hit Mrs. Pruitt on her leg. Olive had only been at the school for a week but already everything about her was "too much": her cheeks were too pink; her ponytails were too perky; her glasses were too thick; and she was too helpful. Also her nose was almost permanently blocked so she had to breathe through her mouth.

"Olive," said Mrs. Pruitt, rubbing her thigh, "if you could try not to be so vigorous…"

Beatrice Hunter and her friend Nelisiwe Majola both snorted with laughter and then pretended that they were having a coughing fit.

Olive said, "Sorry, Mrs. Pruitt, I didn't intend to hurt you." She walked to the back of the classroom.

Please don't come and stand next to me, thought Mercy, desperate not to attract any attention. But Olive walked straight towards her, squeezed in beside her, sniffed loudly, and adjusted her glasses.

Mercy moved quietly sideways so she'd be hidden by Olive if Mrs. Pruitt started scanning for volunteers. She had her excuse ready: she'd left her music at home and would bring it the next day. But the excuse wasn't needed because Mrs. Pruitt said: "Beatrice and Nelisiwe, if you are going to laugh at other people's misfortune, you can go first."

Beatrice gave a little yelp of joy and skipped to the front with her sleek blonde ponytail swinging. Nelisiwe walked slowly as if she couldn't really be bothered and slipped a CD into the machine. They stood with their hands on their hips; one white, one black; both tall and strong and, to Mercy, both terrifying.

As they waited for the music to start, Nelisiwe kicked off her shoes and pushed out her chest. She was one of the first girls in the class to wear a bra and Mercy suspected that she liked everyone to notice. Beatrice undid her ponytail and shook her hair free so it fell in a lovely blonde curtain about her shoulders. Beatrice had the kind of face that everyone looked at; you couldn't help it. The previous year in Grade 5 she had caused a major commotion when she'd come to school with highlights in her hair.

"I can't help it if it's natural," she'd said, tossing it about. "My hair just goes this way in the sun."

Once, at the supermarket, Mercy had spotted Beatrice in the bread aisle wearing makeup. Since then Mercy worried about who was going to teach her about makeup when she got a bit older. Aunt Mary had just a pot of Vaseline and a hairbrush on her dressing table. At least Aunt Flora had a box of face powder with a floppy sponge the color of raw chicken. She dabbed this powder on her nose and then wound up her one tube of coral lipstick that she applied to her lips—and sometimes her top teeth— on special occasions.

The song that Beatrice and Nelisiwe put in the CD player came belting out at top volume. *Don't cha wish your girlfriend was hot like me?* They waggled their hips and tossed their heads.

But they only got as far as the chorus when Mrs. Pruitt shouted: "OFF! Switch it OFF!" She held her head in both hands. "Folk dancing," she said, "is dancing done to traditional music. It is not boogying about like disco bunnies. Nelisiwe, you could have done some nice Zulu dancing."

"*Kodwa ndingumXhosa,*" said Nelisiwe. She and Beatrice giggled.

"Oh well, if you're Xhosa, some nice Xhosa dancing then. I mean, is this so hard? Someone come and do me some proper traditional dancing and put me out of my misery."

Mercy held her breath and looked down: "Not me... not me...not me." She pushed the thought out with all her strength. "*I demand that the order be held pending the process.*"

"Janice Matthews," said Mrs. Pruitt and Mercy exhaled.

Janice slunk to the front of the class. She was the tallest girl in the class by miles, although she hunched her shoulders up around her ears. She stood on one leg with an arm raised above her head, looking like a gloomy heron. There was a drum roll and then a sound like screaming cats came wailing out of the CD player.

Everyone flinched and covered their ears. It was bagpipes, which Mercy recognized because one of Aunt Flora's favorite records was *Songs of the Western Isles*–the one that made her hit her chest with her fist in time to the music.

Janice rose up on her toes and began to jig about, dancing on the spot.

Jump, jump, point to the ground, point to the knee, jumpy jump.

Beatrice started clapping in time to the music. Then Nelisiwe. Soon half the class was clapping along and smirking at Janice. Nelisiwe had to suck her lips in to stop herself from laughing out loud.

Mercy could sense Olive's alarm beside her. Olive was looking from Janice to Mrs. Pruitt and from Mrs. Pruitt back to Janice as if she was watching tennis. But Mrs. Pruitt did nothing to stop the clapping or the jumpity-jump dancing.

"Thank *goodness*," breathed Olive when Janice eventually stormed over to the CD player and punched stop.

"Why did you stop?" asked Mrs. Pruitt. "That was excellent, Janice. And everyone seemed to be enjoying it. Did your parents show you how to do Scottish dancing?"

"No," said Janice. "I taught myself off YouTube."

"Well, it was marvelous, Janice. Do you see what a rich cultural heritage we have here, class? Here we are, just a small city on the southern tip of Africa and just in this classroom we have Indian, Xhosa, Zulu, Scottish, and Afrikaans...Who's next?"

On the other side of the room, Thando lifted his legs up and down and flapped his elbows like a chicken.

"What are you doing, Thando?" asked Mrs. Pruitt. "You look like a hen."

"It's the funky chicken, Mrs. Pruitt," he said. "The traditional dance of my family."

"Well, stop it."

Thando laughed and did a couple of jerky neck movements to conclude his routine. As he ran his hands through his thick afro, he caught Mercy's eye and she gave him a shy smile then looked down quickly.

"And get a haircut, Thando," said Mrs. Pruitt. "Yolanda, you are next. Please be sensible."

Yolanda strolled to the front of the classroom. She rolled her socks down low, hitched up her skirt and undid a few buttons on her school shirt.

JJ was part of Yolanda's act and his job was music. He hit "play." It was Jack Parrow singing *"Jy dink jy's cooler as ekka"* and Yolanda started to twitch like a robot. JJ's job was to cough whenever a swear word came up.

As ek instep skrikkie hele (COUGH COUGH) bar,
Jy kry nog (COUGH COUGH) geld by jou ma

Mrs. Pruitt soon put a stop to that one as well.

"Don't Afrikaans people have folk dances?" Mrs. Pruitt asked. "What about volkspele? JJ and Yolanda, this is not good enough. I want you to go home and come back with some volkspele."

"I might be Afrikaans, but I'm not a Voortrekker!" said Yolanda.

"Excuse me?" said Mrs. Pruitt.

"We moved here from Pretoria in a car, last year. Not an ox wagon."

"Well for goodness sake, that's what I would expect! But JJ, what about you?"

"I'm not even Afrikaans!" said JJ, looking shocked.

"What are you then?" asked Mrs. Pruitt.

"I dunno. I live in Hayfields," mumbled JJ as if that should explain everything.

Mercy looked at Mrs. Pruitt. She was sitting with her elbows on the desk in front of her, massaging her temples.

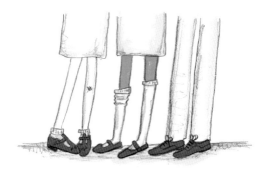

CHAPTER 4

"Right," said Mrs. Pruitt at last. "This is not working so there is a new plan. We're going to get into three groups: Zulu dancers there…" She pointed to a corner of the classroom with one long painted fingernail. "Scottish dancers over there…and Indian dancers over here."

Mercy wanted to join Jameela and her friends who ran quickly to the Indian dancing corner and hopped up and down with excitement. But Mrs. Pruitt put out her hand to stop her. "There will be no other dancing allowed." Then she moved about the class, jostling people into position. And Mercy found herself marched, with Olive, into the Scottish dancing corner where Janice stood by herself picking the edge of her jersey sleeve with her teeth.

All the boys raced over to the Zulu dancing group except for Thando. He took a run up from the far corner and used the slippery soles of his shoes to slide along the floor and bang right into Mercy.

Beatrice too was frog-marched over to join the Scottish dancers. She came rolling her eyes and squeezed in between Olive and Mercy.

"Sorry for being so *vigorous*," she said to Olive. "I didn't *intend* to push you."

Mrs. Pruitt announced that Janice was in charge of Scottish dancers.

Beatrice's arm shot up. "Mrs. Pruitt, actually, can I change? Can I join the Zulu dancers?"

"No, Beatrice, you may not. No swapping between groups. I don't care..." she flapped her hands as if to disperse some imaginary flies buzzing about her head, "...if you are Congolese, Cape Coloured, or Croatian. You'll all do as you are told."

"Thanks a lot, Janice Matthews," said Beatrice under her breath. "Thanks to you, we all get to look like total dorks in front of the whole school on Friday. Doing these retarded jumps with our pointy toes."

"Not *my* fault," said Janice. "It's not like I even wanted you in this group anyway."

"Mrs. Pruitt," said Beatrice. "Janice Matthews says that she doesn't want me in this group, so can I move now?"

"Oh for heaven's sake!" said Mrs. Pruitt. "We only have two days to get this together. Can we be tolerant please?" She glared at Janice and turned her attention back towards the Indian dancers.

"I didn't say that," hissed Janice. "I meant I didn't *choose* you to be in this group." Her eyes filled with tears. She wiped her nose on her sleeve and left a long trail of slime on her jersey.

Beatrice looked around the group with her eyes and mouth wide open. She flashed finger signs on her forehead.

"I am *not* a major loser," said Janice and she burst into tears.

"I did not say you were," said Beatrice.

"You made that...that sign thing on your forehead."

"For your information, I was not making that sign. I was just scratching my forehead. Oh, so is it a rule now that we're not allowed to scratch our foreheads in this group? Well, I s'pose you're in charge, so we just have to listen to you." She shrugged.

Thando put up both his hands. "Woh! Woh! Guys—just hang on," he started.

But Beatrice put her hand on his chest to interrupt him. "OK so these are the rules. From now on we are not allowed to scratch our foreheads, but we do have to scratch the floor with pointy toes like retarded chickens."

Janice made a howling sound and she ran from the classroom, practically knocking over Mrs. Pruitt as she went.

And then the bell rang for break.

CHAPTER 5

Mercy picked up her lunch box from the corridor and walked straight to the library. It was where she went most break times. When she was younger and everyone had played skipping or clapping games, she'd joined in. But these days no one except the boys played games anymore: they sat in little groups and talked. About other people mostly, or about TV series or cell phones, and it was getting harder and harder for Mercy to have anything to say. She didn't have a cell phone, and the TV set, before it got sold at the auction, had lived in the corner of the dining room on a trolley, covered with a green velvet cloth fringed with pom-poms. The last program she had watched about six months ago was a documentary on the Galapagos Islands.

Miss Derby didn't really allow food in the library, but for some reason she made an exception for Mercy. As Mercy lifted the lid of her Tupperware, the image of Aunt Mary and Aunt Flora in their bobbly old dressing gowns at home in the kitchen making her sandwiches made her as sad as the smell of hot plastic and overripe banana: Aunt Mary cutting the crusts off with the broken bread knife and Aunt Flora fussing, fetching the banana and getting in the way and then wrapping the marmite sandwich up tightly in an old used bread bag. There was a time when they'd wrapped sandwiches in wax paper, but these days they recycled everything possible: even tea bags, after their fourth or fifth dunking in boiling water, were put on the veranda to dry and then soaked in paraffin to be used as firelighters in the winter.

Mercy settled into a beanbag in her usual corner under the window when she heard sniffing over in the Fiction section and saw Janice's blonde head sticking out over the stacks. Then she heard Olive asking Miss Derby if she had a book called *The Lion, the Witch, and the Wardrobe*.

"I think it's by a famous author called Cecily Lewis," Olive said so loudly that everyone in the library turned to look at her.

"You'll find it under Lewis in the Fiction section," said Miss Derby with her finger to her lips. "And it's not Cecily Lewis. It's a man called CS Lewis."

Mercy buried herself in a book she'd pulled randomly off the display by the entrance: *The Wonders of the Ocean*. There was a chapter called *Do fish feel pain?* And although she read the same passage over and over, by the end of break time she still didn't know the answer.

CHAPTER 6

The bike Mercy rode to and from school had once belonged to Aunt Mary. It clanked and creaked and when she was perched high on the seat, her feet only just touched the pedals. It felt like riding a very bony, long-horned cow. Everyone else caught taxis or their parents fetched them from school in cars, but Aunt Mary and Aunt Flora had ridden to school as children and believed that Mercy should do the same. The only concession to these modern, more dangerous times was that Mercy had to stick to the pavement and keep off the road, because of the taxis that came flying down Jesmond Road.

"Bye, Mercy. Bye!" called Olive as Mercy wobbled past her out of the school gate. Olive was sitting on a bench in the shade waiting for her mother with her backpack all zipped up at her feet. She reminded Mercy of a little mole with her velvet skin, her small mouth, and her thick glasses. Her uniform was so large and new, it still had creases as if it had just been pulled out of a packet.

Mercy took one hand off the handlebars to wave at her but almost rode into Thando who was right in the middle of a group of boys, all pushing each other and kicking a pale blue ball of scrunched up paper. Mercy recognized the paper ball immediately.

When they'd got back to class after break, Mrs. Pruitt had had a change of heart about the folk dancing.

"If you can't be trusted to behave *properly* and take advantage of *fun* educational opportunities," she'd snapped, "then I'm afraid we will just have to do things where at least I have some control over you." She slapped down a piece of pale blue paper on each desk with the words *"The South African Children's Charter"* written at the top.

"On Friday, *everyone* will hold placards, which I will make."

Mercy realized that Mrs. Pruitt was leaving nothing to chance.

"The placards will have the children's rights printed clearly for the audience to read. *Everyone* will memorize one of the rights for homework. *Everyone* will come to school tomorrow for the rehearsal wearing PT shorts and plain T-shirts in one of the colors of the South African flag." And then she underlined the words *blue, red, green, black,* and *white* so many times that her chalk broke.

Beatrice had put up her hand. "So are you saying we can't wear pale pink, Mrs. Pruitt? It's just that some of us look better in pastels."

Mrs. Pruitt hadn't bothered to answer. She'd marched up and down the line of desks with a red pen, marking everyone's words to be memorized for homework.

Bending over Mercy's desk, she'd underlined the words: *All children have the right to a safe, secure. and nurturing family and the right to participate as a member of that family.* Then she asked Mercy in a quiet voice to please sit next to Thando and help him.

"Mrs. Pruitt says I can help you memorize your words," Mercy said, moving her chair alongside his. "She thinks two heads will be better than one."

"Well, only if those heads are not on the same body." Thando laughed as he tilted back in his chair with his hands behind his head.

Thando had been in their class a few months and although he'd spent years in the remedial unit, he still struggled to read. But there were "no flies on him," which was an expression Mercy had learned from Aunt Mary, who declared often that there were no flies on her either. When he'd first arrived in the class, Nelisiwe and Beatrice had tried to knock him down: "Mrs. Pruitt, how do you spell *remedial?*" they had asked, looking puzzled. "Does *unintelligent* have two 'l's' or one?" But Thando had just ignored them. He was like a ball pushed under the water. No matter how many times he got pushed down, he bounced up again.

"OK, wait, I can do this," he said to Mercy that afternoon, gripping the blue paper in both hands.

"*All...child-ren, children...have...the rig-ht...rig-hit?* That sounds wrong." He scratched his head and looked at Mercy.

"It's *'right,'*" said Mercy. "'*All children have the right to be protected from all types of violence including physical, emotional, verbal, psychological, domestic...*'"

"Hectic," he said. "So many kinds of violence?" Then he scrunched the paper up into a ball and tapped it on his foot as if it was a tiny football. There was no way he was going to read, let alone learn, all those words.

CHAPTER 7

Mercy flew down the pavement of Jesmond Road with the bike rattling. Most of the houses were behind vibracrete walls with metal spikes along the top. There were places along the home route that she liked, like the big flat lawn in front of the Full Gospel Church, and some that scared her so much that she stood up on the pedals and passed them as quickly as she could. One had a sign on the gate saying, "Do you believe in life after death? Enter this property and find out." There was a picture of a dog with its teeth bared and spit flying. Another one had a picture of a cobra with its hood out ready to strike. It just said, "Beware!" Mercy flew over concrete driveways, the place of deviltjie thorns, the place where white ants had eaten away most of the grass, and the place where the sewage leaked and made the grass green all year round and the ground squelchy.

She had to hop off her bike for the last stretch; it was too steep to turn the corner into Hodson Road, although she always tried till her legs ached and the bike started to topple.

She could see home as she turned the corner. But then

she imagined the social worker doing a "home circumstances visit" and tried to look at Number 7 Hodson Road with her eyes.

"No fence or wall. No spikes, no security gate. No guard dog. No burglar alarm," the social worker would sigh and make notes on her official form.

Mercy had to wheel her bike around a pile of lemons that Aunt Flora had put out on the pavement for people to help themselves to if they wanted. Some had rolled into the road, squashed flat by cars. "Food lying on the road," Mercy imagined the social worker writing on the clipboard. "Attracting flies."

But even the fussiest social worker would have to agree that the house, peeping out from behind the overgrown garden, had a friendly face. It wore a red brick skirt, and it had white walls and a deep veranda. Like all good houses, it had a chimney. The roof was tiled and covered in lichen and only if you looked closely could you see the paint peeling off the wooden windows.

Chaining the bike to the pole that supported the carport under the camel's foot tree, Mercy heard piano playing and Aunt Flora's warbling voice through the open bay window:

"One MEATball, one MEATball..."

What would the social worker write about that? Would there be a question on the form that asked, "Is this child being brought up in a home with people who are completely normal?"

She ran up the crazy-paving path fringed by sword ferns, up the red painted steps to the stoep, and opened the door that was never locked during the day.

"The waiter bellowed through the hall
You get no bread with ONE me-e-e-eat ball!"

Aunt Flora did a tinkling flourish on the piano just as Mercy closed the door behind her.

She felt as if she'd just outrun a monster and got away.

CHAPTER 8

The house had the familiar smell of furniture oil and blue mottled soap but Mercy still could not get used to the emptiness of the rooms. It had been months since the auctioneers had loaded up most of the furniture to be sold, but every time she opened that front door, she still got a shock.

What would the social worker say about this lack of furniture? Would they lose points if they only had a small flap of off-cut carpet instead of the lovely old red and blue runner that used to lie in the hall? Would it matter if they didn't have matching sofas and chairs anymore? Or pictures? What would happen if the social worker sat in one of the horrible chairs and the springs poked her bottom? Maybe the piano that stood in golden afternoon sun in the bay window would earn them some points.

Aunt Flora beamed at her. "Mercy, dear. Lovely. *Lovely.*" She patted Mercy's cheek and twinkled as she passed her in the hall.

"Mary!" she called. "Mercy is home for..." but she appeared to have forgotten the word for *tea.*

When the furniture had gone from the house, random words from Aunt Flora's vocabulary had gone too: *visitors, clocks, potatoes* and now *tea.* They just disappeared.

As Mercy walked down the cool, dark passage, she could just make out the pictures that hung in the darkness: it was only the fact that they were family photographs that had stopped them from being sold on the auction. Her favorite was one of Aunt Flora and Aunt Mary's parents on their wedding day. The bride was tiny and covered from head to foot in lace and the tall groom wore a black suit with white flaps covering his shoes. Aunt Mary told her they were called spats and Mercy had thought for years that he'd spat on his shoes to make them shiny for the wedding. There were lots of relatives and three fat bridesmaids; one wore glasses. One looked a lot like Aunt Mary. No one smiled. Then there was another photo that looked as if it had been colored in with crayons: Aunt Mary and Aunt Flora as children at the beach with their mother and father. They had bare feet, rosy cheeks, and striped dresses, but their father wore a shirt and tie and their mother wore a cardigan, lace-up shoes, and a straight face. There was only one photo of Mercy: a school portrait from Grade 1. Her hair was tied up in tight bunches and she had no front teeth.

In her room she took off her hot socks and shoes, and felt the cool clay tiles under her feet with relief. A bee was buzzing against the louvered glass of her bedroom window, so she pulled a metal lever to open the slats and hoped that it would zoom off into the garden. But it didn't. It scrabbled with its tiny legs, trying to climb the glass, but kept falling back onto the window ledge. So she cupped her hands around it to help it find the opening. Aunt Flora once kept bees in the garden and had taught Mercy to be calm when she saw one. "They are gentle creatures," Aunt Flora told her. "They just want to get on and do their work, unless you threaten them; only then, you have to be careful."

Outside, under her bedroom window, her chicken called Lemon was scuffling about in the dry leaves of the petria bush until suddenly, as if a new thought had just occurred to her, she set off for the boundary fence between the garden and the vacant plot next door, with her head bobbing. Mercy had raised her since she was just a tiny lemon-sized ball and now she was a big, white hen and not lemony in color or shape at all. She used to lay her eggs in a cardboard box outside the kitchen, but it had been weeks since Mercy had found an egg there. Perhaps if she hurried she'd be able to see where Lemon was laying. It was probably on the vacant plot.

The vacant plot had once been part of the large garden of Number 7 Hodson Road. A few years back, when money had started to become a problem, Aunt Mary had tried to sell it. But it had turned out that a whole lot of money was needed to pay a surveyor to come and measure it and then a whole lot more money to get it registered before Aunt Mary could sell it—so the sale had never happened. Their neighbor Mr. de Wet, who lived over the road, put up the fence to mark off the new smaller garden and the plot soon became overgrown with tall kikuyu grass, bug weed, and lantana. A huge bougainvillea had twined its way round the wild pear tree that rose above the weeds, and when it flowered in September every year, it looked like the tree had made two types of flowers: bright pink and white.

Aunt Mary had been relieved when the fence had gone up because it meant that she only needed to weed and mow the garden around the house. But Aunt Flora could not get used to the change and sometimes she'd take the secateurs and go and cut a bunch of azaleas or hydrangeas, and then she'd come back into the house, confused.

"There was a great bank of hydrangeas just there." She would point over the fence. "Have they been stolen? And where is the fountain? Don't you remember, Mercy? The big old fountain? Did they take that as well?" Aunt Flora believed recently that thieves had stolen everything: gravel paths, herbaceous borders, bee hives, big pieces of lawn, fountains—all the parts of the garden that were no longer there but had been once, when she'd been a girl.

Mercy climbed through the fence, careful not to snag her school uniform on the barbed wire.

"Puck, Puck, Puckaaak..." she clucked but there was no sign of Lemon, so she picked her way with bare feet, avoiding the dog poo, the bees, and the thistles and went and stood under the wild pear and looked at the blue sky through the branches. She could hear the soft buzz of bees above.

Their gentle hum was drowned out by the roar of an engine. A big silver 4X4 with steel bars ramped the pavement and parked. Then a man with a pink face, wearing a tight grey suit and pointed shoes, got out and slammed the door. He had a cell phone clenched between his shoulder and his cheek and he carried a pen and notebook in his hand. He walked around the edges of the plot with big steps, counting as he went...

"...about one twenty, one thirty. Ball park estimates... Ja."

Then he swore and lifted up his foot, dropped his phone, and swore again. "Sorry," he said to whoever he was talking to, while he wiped his shoe on the grass. "Just dealing with some kak here."

Mercy sat on her haunches behind an old beehive. For some reason, she didn't want the man with the pink face to see her.

CHAPTER 9

"How is that poor Mrs. Pruitt?" asked Aunt Mary as she planted a firm kiss on the top of Mercy's head. "Did you give her the note?"

"It's not poor Mrs. Pruitt. It's poor me," Mercy replied. "The dancing thing didn't work out. So we're doing the Children's Charter and I have to memorize something about children's rights." She screwed up her nose.

"Would you rather have danced?" asked Aunt Mary, surprised.

"No."

"Then you got a lucky escape." She scrubbed a potato in the sink with a bald old scrubbing brush. "Be glad and free and exercise your right to say 'no thank you' if you wish."

The problem was Mercy had said "no thank you" a lot recently. For instance the week before, as she was leaving for school, Mr. de Wet's dog Duke had escaped from his front garden and chased Lemon down Hodson Road, snapping at her tail feathers. Lemon had flown into a tree, but by the time Mercy had fetched her down, she was frozen in terror, her eyes shut tight and her whole body trembling. Aunt Mary fetched an old towel and together they wrapped

Lemon in it and sat with her in the morning sun, stroking her and feeding her sugar water with a dropper. Calming the chicken had taken a few hours.

Mrs. Pruitt did not think that nursing a shocked chicken was a good excuse to miss a geography test and complained to Aunt Mary on the phone. But Aunt Mary disagreed.

"I will never allow something as silly as *going to school* to get in the way of your education, Mercy," Aunt Mary said when she put the phone down.

If the social worker got to hear about that, Mercy knew that there would be trouble. But there were other things, of course, to worry about as well.

The tea, for example, that was waiting on the enamel-topped kitchen table was looking poor, almost pitiful: just the tea-pot, sugar, and plain Albany brown bread. No butter, no jam, no biscuits. No milk. A social worker would notice things like that.

"Do we have something to put on the bread?" Mercy asked.

"Yes, the last nice ripe avocado," said Aunt Mary. She disappeared into the scullery but returned empty handed.

Aunt Flora stirred four spoons of sugar into her tea and nibbled a slice of bread. Beside her plate was a lump of a parcel, something oval and wrapped in many layers of packet and tied with string.

"Flora," said Aunt Mary, looking out the kitchen window, "has the post come yet? I'm waiting for that letter."

"I'll just pop out and look," said Aunt Flora. She pushed back her chair and hurried outside.

Aunt Mary unwrapped the avocado from the packet.

Mercy sat really still. She had a hot feeling behind her eyes that required a lot of blinking to make it go away.

Everything went blurry and she could not swallow.

"Mercy? Sweetheart?" said Aunt Mary. "Dear child, are you all right?"

Mercy fought the feeling for as long as she could. But eventually two hot, fierce little tears came out—and there was nothing she could do to stop them.

CHAPTER 10

Aunt Mary sat on Mercy's bed with her and gave her a big handkerchief to blow her nose.

"It's called Alzheimer's," she said. "And a book I read explained what is happening to Flora like this: when you think something, it's as if your thoughts travel along a little road in your brain and they get to their destination easily. So you can remember words, people's faces, what you have to do for homework, how to get home from school by yourself..." She sat close, rubbing Mercy's back with her big warm hand.

"But with Flora, it's as if her roads are blocked. Some of the roads in her brain have closed. Some streets have become one-ways, some roads that used to be busy free-ways are now cul-de-sacs. There are lots of pot-holes and dead ends. It's like trying to get to the library in town when they were laying that dratted paving outside the city hall. Do you remember?"

Mercy nodded. She knew that if she tried to talk, she'd cry again.

"So her thoughts just can't get through like they used to. Sometimes she has to go on a long, windy route to get to where she wants to go. Those back roads sometimes take her very close to her destination, but not *quite* there. This morning she wanted a broom to sweep up the leaves and she asked for something to sweep up the 'flutterings.'" Aunt Mary chuckled.

"And I'm afraid slowly more and more roads in her brain are going to close. But the roads that were laid down years ago are not as badly damaged as the more recent ones. So she remembers things that happened fifty years ago better than what happened yesterday."

"Do we have to tell the social worker?" Mercy tried to make the question sound as if she'd just thought of it. But as soon as she said it, she worried that it sounded too casual.

"Oh no." Aunt Mary waved her hand. "We don't need to tell those interfering old turnips. We'll manage quite well on our own although it won't be easy. Life, as one of my favorite authors says, is sometimes sad and often dull. But there are currants in the cake..." She rummaged deep in her pocket. "And here is one of them. Close your eyes and hold out your hand."

She put something cold and solid in Mercy's palm. When Mercy opened her eyes she saw a small brass bird which she covered with her other hand to keep it safe.

"Thanks," she whispered.

"I did some work at Hospice today sorting stuff and someone brought in a whole box of ornaments. Do you want to put it with your collection?"

Mercy pulled out a shoebox from the pine bedside table next to her bed and they looked at her collection of birds together: birds of all shapes and sizes made from wood, glass, brass and beads nesting in cotton wool and some of

Lemon's white feathers.

Aunt Mary reached for a walnut shell in which two tiny carved birds nested in blue checked gingham. She dangled the little nest from its red silk loop off her finger. "This used to hang on our Christmas tree," she said.

Mercy picked up two big ceramic birds' heads that looked as if they were once lids for jars. The pottery made a clunking sound when the two heads touched. They had comical faces, big beaks, and sly slit eyes.

"Those were the lids for tobacco jars," said Aunt Mary. "My mother gave them to my father." She took one of the heads, held it up to her nose, and inhaled deeply.

"Extraordinary. I can still smell the tobacco. I wonder what happened to the jars?" Aunt Mary sat still with a far-away look in her eyes.

"Smells are like a portal to the past," she said. "I smell that tobacco and my own father is standing here before me. He did love his pipe tobacco." She looked at her watch. "Good gracious! Is that the time? I'd better go and look for Flora. I think I saw her under the pecan nut tree cooing at the pigeons."

Alone now, Mercy picked up the birds' heads and breathed in the faint warm smell of tobacco. It was a clean smell like soil or the furniture polish that Aunt Flora used to rub into the old table before it was taken away by the auctioneers. She ran her fingers over the birds in the shoe-box and picked up a key ring that belonged to her mother Rose. Her Aunty Kathleen, her mother's sister, had given it to Mercy as a keepsake. It was a flat, flexible ribbon of beads, and the Yale key to the small flat in Nedbank Plaza, where Mercy had lived with her mother for five years, was still attached. She ran her fingers over the beaded ridges and traced the outline of the bird that looked like a long-legged flamingo that was woven into the pattern. She remembered very little of that flat: the metallic taste of the iron railings on the tiny balcony and the damp patch on the bathroom ceiling that looked like a scary man with a long chin. She remembered going back there after her mother died, with Aunty Kathleen holding tightly onto her hand—and Uncle Clifford, who was married to Aunty Kathleen, stuffing Mercy's pink princess duvet cover and clothes into a black bin bag and slamming drawers and cupboard doors. Mercy remembered the dark bulk of his frame storming ahead of them down the unlit corridor to the lift with the bin bag over his shoulder. Aunty Kathleen had lifted Mercy onto her hip, kissed her cheek, and said, "Don't worry about him, my baby. Everything will be fine."

Mercy held the key to her nose and breathed in. But it yielded no smell—apart from the slightly coppery odor of wire.

CHAPTER 11

A few days later, the man in the tight grey suit appeared again. This time they nearly ran him over.

Aunt Mary was reversing out of the driveway in the old yellow car as she always did—by staring straight in front of her because her neck was too stiff to swivel. Aunt Flora was in the passenger seat and it was Mercy's job to sit on her haunches looking out the back window for cars, people, dogs and hens.

But as they shot down the driveway and swung backwards into Hodson Road, the man appeared from nowhere, hitting the roof of the car with the flat of his hand to get Aunt Mary to stop.

"Hells Bells!" said Aunt Flora. "Did we run someone over?"

The man stuck his hot, pink face inside the car and Aunt Mary had to flatten herself against the seat to get away from him. Mercy remembered that he'd stepped in dog poo a few days before and hoped he'd cleaned his shoes.

"I'm looking for Mrs. Knight. Does she live here?"

"*Miss McKnight,*" said the aunts together.

"And yes, we both live here," said Aunt Mary.

"Mrs. McNutt, how do you do?" Mercy noticed the sweaty patches around his armpits as he reached his warm clammy hand into the car to shake each of their hands. She quickly wiped her hand on her T-shirt.

"I'm Mr. Craven from Boyce, Craven, and Associates. I have a business proposal—."

"Well, Mr. Craven, as you can see, we are going out. Off to the supermarket."

"I'll leave you my card," said Mr. Craven, and he slapped his pockets and fished out a small card.

"Good afternoon, Mr. Craven," said Aunt Mary, driving off. She handed Mercy the business card over her shoulder.

"Boyce, Craven, and Associates, Specialist Developers of Cluster Housing," Mercy read off the card.

"Cluster Housing. Pish!" said Aunt Mary. "As if we'd be interested in cluster housing. And imagine trying to interest us in a business proposal out on the pavement."

When they got to the Nedbank Plaza, Aunt Flora scurried ahead, hugging a parcel and her handbag to her chest.

"Just keep an eye on her, sweetheart," said Aunt Mary as she locked the car.

Mercy had to walk fast to keep up. She was wearing slipslops that were too big for her and they made an embarrassing slap on the tiles of the shopping center floor. Aunt Mary believed in buying things Mercy could grow into, but sometimes Mercy really wished for something that wasn't secondhand and was just the right size.

Aunt Flora went straight into a shoe shop and unwrapped the parcel on the counter. Inside all the old newspaper was a single shoe: black with a little heel.

"I wonder if you could help me," Aunt Flora said to a

shop assistant. "I have lost one of my shoes and I need to buy another one. I don't need *two* new shoes because as you can see I already have one. Can I just buy *one* shoe in this size?"

The shop assistant looked around her, confused.

"What?" she said rudely.

Aunt Flora repeated her story.

"No," said the shop assistant, speaking slowly and loudly. "We only sell two shoes at a time. They always come in pairs."

Mercy put her hand on Aunt Flora's arm to try and get her to leave the shop, but she gave an impatient shrug and clung to the counter.

"That's just wasteful," she said, looking as if she might cry. "What am I going to do with this one shoe? I have two feet."

"Come, Flora," said Aunt Mary when she'd caught up with them. She took the shoe and put it in the pocket of her dress.

"So sorry to worry you," she said to the shop assistant and she took hold of Mercy's hand and looped her arm through Aunt Flora's arm and steered them out of the shop.

"You're rushing me," complained Aunt Flora. "I just want..."

"Want what, dear?"

"I want...you know."

"I do know," said Aunt Mary. "You want two shoes."

"Exactly," said Aunt Flora. "I want to choose...I want to choose who I talk to and what I do. And I don't want you bossing me all the time."

Aunt Mary squeezed Mercy's hand a bit tighter. Mercy looked up at her and saw her smile, but for the first time she noticed too how tired Aunt Mary looked.

CHAPTER 12

It was almost dark when they got home from the supermarket. Mercy went around the house making sure that the curtains were properly drawn. They had to meet exactly in the middle so that no one looking in from outside would be able to see even a chink of light.

The groceries made a very small pile on the kitchen table. Aunt Mary had studied every onion and counted every banana and practically every bean that had gone into the trolley. They'd bought a giant box of no-name brand tea bags, milk powder, a bag of dried beans and a bag of soup bones but tiny bits of everything else: three lamb chops as a treat for supper, a small bag of sugar, a single bar of soap, one long life light bulb.

Mercy had looked at the contents of other trolleys while they waited in line to pay. Some people bought tubs of chocolate yogurt, fabric softener, crumbed chicken, and three different kinds of cheese. They handed over their credit cards without even looking at how much everything cost. Mercy had hardly been able to watch as Aunt Mary paid, counting out the notes with her stiff fingers and emptying the coins into her cupped hand to give over the exact amount.

"Well," said Aunt Mary as they packed the food away in the cupboard and the fridge, "there's no fillet steak or *foie gras*. But we'll survive." She washed her hands and started scraping at a floppy carrot she'd found at the bottom of the fridge.

"When will this war be over?" asked Aunt Flora. "I'm so tired of food rations. I'm going to make a cake. Mrs. Morris made us a cake last week. Do you know what she did, Mercy? She didn't have any butter so she used *liquid paraffin*! I'm going to make us a nice paraffin cake."

Bang! Bang! Bang!

The noise of the brass knocker on the front door exploded through the house, shocking as gunshot.

Aunt Mary put down the scraping knife, wiped her hands on a tea towel, and went to investigate. Mercy heard the click of the light switch in the hall.

Her mouth went dry with fear. Did social workers make house calls at this time of day? From the kitchen, she heard a man's voice and Aunt Mary saying, "I'm afraid this also isn't a good time."

Aunt Flora wandered through to the scullery to scuffle amongst the plastic packets. Mercy wanted to be near a grown up but it was dark in the scullery since Aunt Mary had unscrewed the light bulb to use in the hall, so she crept into the passage to be nearer to Aunt Mary.

She peeped around the corner. It was Mr. Craven again! He leaned with one arm on the doorframe.

She ducked out of sight in the passage and stood listening with her forehead pressed to the cool wall.

"No," he said. "We must have both....The vacant land on its own is too small."

"But Mr. Craven, we *live* here. And this house is not for

sale." Aunt Mary enunciated each word as if he was a bit deaf.

"Well, Mrs. McNutt, everyone has their price. If you could just hear me out..."

"No, you hear *me* out, Mr. Craven. My sister and I have lived in this house for over sixty-five years and we have no intention whatsoever of moving out."

"Well, if I could just give you these...you could read them at your leisure."

There was a short pause.

"Thank you. Now good evening, Mr. Craven."

And she shut the door.

Mercy heard Aunt Mary open the drawer of the little desk that they used as a phone table in the hall. She slipped quickly back into the kitchen before Aunt Mary saw her.

It was very hard to eat supper that evening. The lamb chop was very tough and it took many gulps of water for each mouthful to go down. But what bothered Mercy even more was that Aunt Mary said nothing about Mr. Craven and what he wanted. She kept waiting for Aunt Mary to say something, but there was just the sound of their knives and forks scraping. Even Aunt Flora was silent; she was so busy chewing her chop. She kept putting more and more food into her mouth until her cheeks were bulging, but hard as she chewed, the ball of food refused to go down. She looked desperate and her eyes filled with tears.

"You don't have to eat that, Flora dear," said Aunt Mary eventually. "It's so tough; more ram chop than lamb chop, if you ask me." Aunt Flora spat it carefully in her hanky and tucked it into her cardigan sleeve.

Later, after she'd done her homework and read her library book, Mercy saw that Aunt Mary was washing the supper plates. She crept back to the hall even though she hated the black window above the door that had no curtain. She imagined a tall man on long legs looking in from outside. She opened the drawer of the phone table. There were two pamphlets lying on top of the telephone directory: one was a glossy brochure showing a small drawing of little beige box houses. Half a page was taken up with a photograph of a family snuggling up together on a sofa with a puppy. She read: *Craven, Boyce, and Associates Cluster housing, 12 units! Exciting new family oriented development! Affordable! Become part of our vision!*

The other was for an Old Age Home at the bottom of West Street called Evergreen Park. There were two photographs: cleaners in overalls and a caption that read, *Our happy cleaners keep things spic and span,* and a close-up of a pink rose. Mercy had visited Aunt Flora's friend Mrs. Mullins who lived in an Old Age Home near the freeway and she'd never seen any cheerful cleaners or roses—just rooms with low ceilings, dark corridors, and old ladies wrapped in knitted blankets watching TV. There was one old lady who chewed constantly, although she had nothing in her mouth, and an old man who walked round and round the paved courtyard slapping his arms and pulling his hair. The place smelled of cooked mince and something that reminded her of the boys' toilets at school.

She stuffed both pamphlets back in the drawer.

When Aunt Mary came to say goodnight, she turned Mercy's pillow over onto the cool side and laid a hand gently on her head, as she did every night. Mercy held onto that hand tightly, hoping Aunt Mary would stay sitting quietly on the edge of her bed. But Aunt Flora came shuffling in in her dressing gown. "I'm looking for the bathroom," she

said. "It's disappeared." So Aunt Mary released her hand
and went to guide Aunt Flora down the passage and to run
her bath.

Sleep was a long time coming and when it came, it
writhed like a snake pit full of terrible dreams. Mercy was
in a locked room but through the window she could see
her mother Rose, dead and floating weightless in the
sky. Outside the room, her Uncle Clifford was shouting
and throwing things against the door. "Rose is dead!" he
shouted. "It was Rose who did this to me! Just one mistake
and now I have to look at this child forever."

"Mercy is just a baby," she heard her Aunty Kathleen
crying. "It's not her fault!"

It was only in the early morning, as the birds began
to sing, that Aunt Mary arrived out of the darkness and
took Mercy away from all the shouting. Mercy clung to her
neck as Aunt Mary carried her to the yellow car and away
to a long and peaceful sleep. There were doves in the trees
and the sound of leaves rustling. And Aunt Mary said that
she never needed to see her Uncle Clifford or listen to his
shouting again.

CHAPTER 13

"Speak UP, Mercy!" Mrs. Pruitt roared. "You have to PROJECT YOUR VOICE." She made huge movements with her arms from where she was standing near the back of the hall.

But if Mrs. Pruitt was hoping that her voice, rolling out like magnificent thunder, would pick up Mercy's voice and carry it all the way to the back of the hall, it wasn't working.

Mrs. Pruitt had made placards for everyone. On the audience side of each card, "The Rights" were spelled out in thick black paint: *I have the right to be protected. I have the right to say no to violence. I have the right to education.* Mercy's placard read: *I have the right to a safe family life.* On the back of each one, Mrs. Pruitt had taped the full script, so that if someone hadn't learned their lines, they could just read off the words. In this way, she hoped to avoid disasters.

But Mercy could see already that this wasn't working: for example, Thando reserved the right not to say his sentence at all, although Mrs. Pruitt had already shortened it to: *All children have the right to be protected from violence.*

"I have the right to say NO!" he said loudly, no matter how much Mrs. Pruitt told him that he had to say the whole sentence.

"Thando, you are being very difficult. Aren't you excited to appear in front of the whole school and take assembly?" asked Mrs. Pruitt.

"I'm not excited yet, Mrs. Pruitt. But I'm sure it will hit me soon," he said.

Mrs. Pruitt slapped her thigh with her paper and turned her attention to Yolanda who was sitting on the stage steps examining the split ends in her ponytail. JJ was brandishing Yolanda's placard like a lightsaber, swishing it through the air and making electronic whooshing noises.

"Stop it, JJ," said Mrs. Pruitt. She had a dangerous edge to her voice.

Yolanda took back her placard, puffed air through her lips, and read: *"All children have the right to be protected by maltreatment, neglect, and abuse..."*

"Excuse me?" interrupted Mrs. Pruitt.

"All children have the right to be protected by maltreatment..."

"What does that *mean* exactly? How can you be protected by maltreatment and neglect? Do you even understand what you are reading?"

Yolanda looked again at the script taped to the back of her placard. "Protected *from* maltreatment, neglect, and abuse." Then under her breath: *"From, by, whatever..."*

"No, it's not 'whatever,' Yolanda. Those words are called prepositions and they matter. They really affect the meaning of things. But...oh, why am I even bothering with this?" Mrs. Pruitt turned away and walked to the back of the hall where she stood with her back to the class and rested her head against the climbing bars, her thin arms hanging at her side.

Everyone was silent.

Mercy turned around to look for someone to rescue the situation and help bring Mrs. Pruitt back to life. But Beatrice and Nelisiwe, on the back step near the stage, high fived each other without making a sound: if Mrs. Pruitt was going to have a nervous breakdown, they sensed a free lesson and they were going to start their celebrations right away.

Mrs. Pruitt walked out and Mercy heard the door to the toilet at the back of the hall hiss and thud behind her.

Nelisiwe started a quiet toyi toyi on the steps, lifting her knees high and punching the air with her right fist raised. In her other hand, she waved her placard. Beatrice joined in and their bare feet made a gentle rhythmic thumping on the floorboards. The rhythm was infectious and soon others began to punch the air with clenched fists in time with the quiet beat.

Olive, who was standing next to Mercy, looked wide-eyed and terrified. She was staring straight ahead with her blue T-shirt well tucked into her PE shorts, holding her placard in front of her like a shield. She'd attached herself to Mercy since she'd arrived at school that morning, like one of those wingless flying ants that trails around on the floor, holding onto the bottom of the flying ant in front.

Thando bounded up the steps and waved his arm in front of his face. "Hey guys! Stop!" But this just seemed to encourage them and their knees lifted higher and their fists tightened.

Thando jabbed Nelisiwe with his placard and when she still didn't stop, he swung it, just missing her face—and just as he did so, Mrs. Pruitt walked in.

"Thando!"

"Sorry, ma'am. I was just..." He raised his arms.

"You were just what, Thando? Just going to brain some-one with that placard? I can't deal with you today. I'm giving you a demerit. Make that two. And if you complain, you'll get three. And if anyone gives me any trouble for the rest of this lesson, they will get one too. Now out. Out! Go to Mrs. Griesel." She flapped her hands.

Thando put his placard down and walked out.

Olive nudged Mercy in the ribs. "Go and tell her," she whispered. "It's not fair. She needs to *know*." Olive looked around to glare at Beatrice.

Mercy felt a sharp sting on her ear and a rubber band fell at her feet. She whipped her head round and saw Beatrice standing very straight and tall and her mouth was twitching.

The rehearsal continued without incident. Everyone did as they were told. When Mrs. Pruitt told them that the big ending to their performance would be to link arms and sing, *"We are the world, we are the children,"* no-one even complained, although Mercy could imagine Thando gagging when he discovered Mrs. Pruitt's idea of a rousing finale.

"So flat!" said Mrs. Pruitt. "Come on, give it a little oomph."

The placards were heavy to carry upright for so long and by the time they'd finished the rehearsal, they were all dragging on the ground.

As everyone was leaving the hall to go back to class, Olive said, "Excuse me. Excuse me," and pushed through the crowd to talk to Mrs. Pruitt, who was busy propping up the placards against the wall. But Beatrice shoved her aside and tapped Mrs. Pruitt on the shoulder.

"Can I help you carry those to the storeroom, Mrs. Pruitt?" she asked.

"Thank you, Beatrice," said Mrs. Pruitt. "At least there's one child in this class that knows how to behave." She started piling the placards into Beatrice's arms.

Mercy watched as Olive walked away.

CHAPTER 14

Mercy found Thando on the stairwell outside the library. He had a bucket and a scrubbing brush and he was looking up at an expanse of dirty concrete in front of him. Most of the grime was at shoulder height where bodies had pressed against the wall, caught in the bottleneck created by the stairs. Over the years this had made a greasy smear.

"Hello," she said.

"Lo," said Thando.

"Is this your punishment? From Mrs. Griesel?"

"Ja."

"Sorry."

"Nah, it's OK. As my Dad would say: 'You've buttered your bread, now you have to sleep on it.'" He laughed.

Mercy smiled at Thando's habit of twisting words. "I'll help if you want."

"Ja, except..." Thando looked down at the single scrubbing brush in his hand. "I've only got one. Mr. Hartshorne's already locked up the supply room and gone home."

"I'll go home and fetch one. I live close."

Mercy ran to get her bike.

Aunt Flora was picking a frond of sword fern from the path when she got home.

"Mercy, dear, look I have to rescue a little tiny...I think it's a letter of the alphabet." She climbed the red steps and pointed with the frond at her teacup.

Mercy peeped into the teacup and saw a little bee scrabbling around in the sweet milky liquid.

Aunt Flora dipped the fern frond into the teacup and the bee clung on for dear life. "I'm just going to wash it in the fountain," she said, holding the frond and looking left and right with growing confusion.

"Glory be! Where is that fountain? It was here just a minute ago. Has it been stolen? Again?" She sighed and flicked the bee into a clump of cannas. Then it was as if she'd forgotten all about the fountain and the bee.

"Mercy, my dear...hurry and wash your hands. We're going to have...Winnie and Ruby coming. And then we are going to have a lovely walk at the bird sanctuary." She lifted the corner of her cardigan to reveal a brown paper package tucked into the elastic of her tracksuit pants. "And I've got something nice for Winnie for her birthday."

"Mary!" she called down the passage. "We have to hurry. Winnie and Ruby are coming. They're going to be here any minute."

Mercy found Aunt Mary out the back heaving wet sheets onto the washing line. She didn't look as if she was expecting visitors.

"Mercy, sweetheart," said Aunt Mary with a clothes peg in her mouth, "there's something I need to tell you. News."

"I know. Some people called Winnie and Ruby are coming for tea."

"Well, that would be a surprise," said Aunt Mary, "given

that they have both been dead about twenty-five years. They were our friends when we were little girls."

She stopped pegging the sheets and looked into the distance. "We used to play hopscotch with them in our pajamas on the pavement in Victoria Street in the summer."

Mercy could not imagine Aunt Mary playing hopscotch in her pajamas; nor could she imagine Victoria Street as a nice place to play; these days it was so full of supermarkets, car parks, and wholesalers.

"No, the news is, I'm thinking it would be a good idea for us to get a lodger." Aunt Mary wiped her forehead with the back of her hand.

"A lodger?"

"We can fix up that back room over there." Aunt Mary nodded in the direction of the small dark cottage covered in wisteria behind the carport, which was used as a store room. "It's got plumbing and a lavatory. We'll need to paint it of course and install a sink."

Mercy was shocked. She wasn't sure what it would be like to have another person living with them. Having another person around might be another thing to worry about.

"We'll charge some rent," said Aunt Mary. "We can do with a little extra money. It's getting quite difficult to make ends meet these days."

"We're not going to rent it to Mr. Craven, are we?"

Aunt Mary looked surprised and Mercy regretted mentioning his name.

"You remember him? No, we won't be renting it to Mr. Craven. We'll find someone nice."

Someone nice. How would they know if the person was nice?

"We'll get started this weekend. I'll ask Mr. de Wet to help."

Mercy helped Aunt Mary pick up another wet sheet to haul over the clothes-line. "OK," she said. "But I need to borrow a scrubbing brush to help someone at school clean a wall. I have to go back now."

"Under the big sink, I think," said Aunt Mary. "We'll keep some tea for you." Aunt Mary never fussed about where Mercy was or who she was with. Sometimes that bothered Mercy, but today she was glad.

Mercy pulled everything out onto the floor from under the big sink but the scrubbing brush was not there; only a pile of rags and old newspapers, a plastic cup full of old toothbrushes, and an ice cream container on which Aunt Flora had written, "STRING—*pieces too small to be of use.*"

She heard the clunk of the kettle being plonked on the stovetop. Then the screen door slapped and Aunt Mary passed her in the scullery and went into the kitchen.

"Mary, I do things over and over, but they don't stay done," said Aunt Flora.

"What things, dear?"

"I forget," said Aunt Flora.

"I can't find the scrubbing brush anywhere," said Mercy. Aunt Mary looked at Aunt Flora. Aunt Flora looked in the sleeves of her cardigan and found only her hanky.

That scrubbing brush was lost forever, probably wrapped in layers of newspaper and tucked away who knows where. Inside the piano? Inside a shoe? Under a mattress?

"So can I take these old toothbrushes?"

"Of course. And Mercy," she said, scrabbling in her handbag for some money, "if that nice man is still on the corner selling newspapers, will you buy me a Witness?

I need to check on the going rate for garden cottages."

Mercy took the money and went back to school to help Thando clean the wall with old toothbrushes.

CHAPTER 15

"I thought Mrs. Griesel told you to clean the stairwell wall, Thando," said Mrs. Pruitt when she was taking the register.

"I did, Mrs. Pruitt. I cleaned it."

"You only cleaned *bits* of the wall, Thando. What you did was vandalism, not cleaning."

"Not vandalism, Mrs. Pruitt. That's like spray-painting. I was cleaning."

"Thando please, I'm not stupid. It's vandalism. Scratching the word 'NO' on the concrete in four-foot letters is just... insubordinate. And then on the adjacent wall you wrote 'RIGHTS ON WALLS.' What does that mean? If you're going to get clever, you might as well learn to spell."

"I was advertising for you—you know for assembly and all the rights and everything."

"The process of making letters on walls or anywhere is W-R-I-T-E-S. Anyway, assembly is compulsory. It does not need any advertising from you, thank you."

Mrs. Pruitt went to the board and wrote WRITES, RIGHTS, RITES on the board. "Can anyone tell me what we call words like these? Words that are spelled differently but sound the same?"

There was a lot of groaning. Everyone had been enjoying the conversation between Thando and Mrs. Pruitt but they didn't want it to turn into a lesson. Mercy watched Thando, who sat in front right under Mrs. Pruitt's nose, slide lower and lower in his chair until he almost disappeared. While Mrs. Pruitt was writing on the board, he turned around to widen his eyes at her. The spelling of "rights" had been Mercy's idea.

"Anyone?" asked Mrs. Pruitt when the class was silent. "I'll give you a clue. It's a word that starts with an 'H'."

"H-O?"

"H-O-M?"

"H-O-M-O?"

"Homosexual?" Thando volunteered.

Everyone sniggered and Nelisiwe pretended to have the usual coughing fit.

"Honestly," said Mrs. Pruitt and she clicked her tongue against her teeth. "The word is HOMOPHONE." And she wrote it in big letters. "And Thando, you are to stay in at break time and think up a list of homophones for me. And when everyone else goes home, I'm going to personally supervise you while you clean that wall properly and remove that W-R-I-T-I-N-G. "

Thando threw his head back as if he'd been dealt a deadly blow. His eyes rolled back in his head.

Mercy tore off a piece of paper and wrote the first homophones that came to her mind:

pane   pain
board   bored
dam   damn
berry   bury
week   weak

And when they got up to do one last quick practice for the assembly, she slipped the list into Thando's hand.

"Are we passing little love letters?" asked Beatrice who was standing behind them. "Guys! Check this out. Mercy and Thando are passing letters to each other. So cute!"

CHAPTER 16

But after school, Thando was not the only one made to stay behind. Everyone had to wait after the bell because Mrs. Pruitt had a long list of complaints about the class assembly. It had not gone well. Four people had forgotten their lines; someone had pushed Janice off the stage and made her cry; Beatrice had worn tiny cut off denims instead of regulation PT shorts; Thando had just shouted "No!" at the top of his voice; and Mercy had tried to participate, but Mrs. Pruitt claimed she'd heard tiny beetles with voices louder than Mercy's.

"I'm very disappointed," said Mrs. Pruitt. "In all of you."

But there was more...

"Now as you know, we have Parents' Evening coming up at the end of the month," said Mrs. Pruitt.

Mercy didn't know—and the information stabbed her like a needle. Would Aunt Flora and Aunt Mary have to actually come to school? She went hot and prickly just thinking about it.

"Two things I want you to think about," said Mrs. Pruitt. "The theme for Parents' Evening is 'Proudly South African' so we need a big South African flag and some displays showing South African products and inventions. It would be nice if you could all bring South African food to the picnic afterwards."

"What sort of food is that, Mrs. Pruitt?" asked Beatrice. "Because I will not eat Mopani worms."

Everyone went: "Eeeuw!"

"Don't be ridiculous, Beatrice," said Mrs. Pruitt. "There are plenty of delicious South African foods: boerewors sausage, milk tart, frikkadel, Indian samoosas....No one has to eat Mopani worms.

Olive put up her hand to ask a question: "Excuse me, what's a frikkadel?"

"A meatball," said Mrs. Priutt. "You can go home and think about it and we can talk about the food later."

Mercy was already thinking about it. She could see the whole scene in her mind: the parents arriving; fathers and mothers in smart work clothes, slamming the doors of their big silver cars with an expensive thunk. She imagined them chatting and laughing together and the dads setting up skottel braais on the sports field to cook the meat; the folding chairs and the cooler boxes of food. And then she pictured Aunt Mary and Aunt Flora clunking into the car park in the old yellow car, wearing big cotton sun hats and cardigans; Aunt Mary carrying an old bread bag with food for the picnic; Aunt Flora clutching a tightly wrapped parcel and rolling her jersey up from the hem, which is what she did when she got nervous. Mercy could just about hear Aunt Mary telling Mrs. Pruitt about the importance of learning big chunks of poetry off by heart. And then the supper on the sports field. Oh, who would they sit with?

"And the other thing I want you to start thinking about for homework," said Mrs. Pruitt, bringing her back to reality, "is the name of a role model: someone who inspires you. You will need to do an oral on your chosen role model in a few weeks' time. I will give you time in class to go to the library and get organized, but I want you to come to class with a name. You have until the middle of next week to think about it. I want you to really prepare for this. It's a formal assessment and it's a chance to think about what is really important to you, what your values are. "

JJ stuck up his hand. "Do you mean we have to decide between Gisele Bundchen and Candice Swanepoel?"

"Oh for heaven's sake, JJ. I said *role* models, not super models."

"Is there a difference?" JJ looked round and shrugged. Everyone laughed, but Mrs. Pruitt looked grim as she leaned heavily on the desk with her arms.

"Laugh if you like." She looked bored. "And take your time, because you are going to have to think hard to come up with interesting ways of messing this up. In fact, I look *forward* to seeing what kind of a hash you can make with this one. Don't disappoint me!" And she swooped up her books and walked out of the classroom with her head high.

"Teachers at Westmead Primary never spoke to us like that," said Olive to Mercy as they went to collect their bags to go home.

"Well, maybe you should have stayed at Westmead Primary then," said Beatrice. "In fact, why don't you do one of the teachers at Westmead Primary as your role model?"

Olive just blinked at Beatrice through her thick glasses. Her eyes were enormous.

"Guys, guys, guys! Before you all go home..." Beatrice switched her tone of voice as if she'd flicked a switch in her brain. "I forgot I was supposed to hand out these birthday invitations. You have to RSVP," she said, digging in her bag. "'Cuz my mom has to book."

She pulled out a sheaf of invitations and started handing them out. Mercy was surprised to get one. Thando got one. Yolanda got one. Nelisiwe got one, of course...

Mercy noticed that Olive didn't get one.

"Cool," said Nelisiwe. "Thanks. The Wimpy next Friday. I'll come."

"Yay!" said Beatrice. "Nelli, do you want to come and hang out at my house this afternoon? We can start thinking about role models? I'm going to do Miley Cyrus. I've already decided."

"Don't even lie! I was also going to do Miley Cyrus," said Nelisiwe. "But it's cool...I'll do Beyonce instead." They went off arm in arm.

"Cheers, guys," said Thando, stuffing the invitation in his pocket. "Got to do school maintenance. Mrs. Pruitt's waiting for me." He ran off tossing a plastic bottle high in the air and catching it as he went.

"Can I come and do my oral at your house?" Olive looked at Mercy with huge eyes, breathing as she did, through her mouth. "My mom can drop me off. I think I'm going to do Florence Nightingale."

"Florence Nightingale is your role model?"

"Yes. The nurse. Or maybe I'll do Kate what's-her-name. Middleton. What do you think?"

"I don't know."

"So, is it OK if I come to your house?"

Mercy was trapped. She felt as if she was walking around with a basin of water that was full to the very top and it was taking all her concentration to keep that water from slopping out and disappearing down a dark drain. She couldn't have Olive or anyone at her house that weekend.

"Olive," she said, "I'm sorry. This weekend is just..."

But Olive didn't even let her finish. She just turned and walked away in her stiff new dress with her head down. Mercy knew Olive was going to cry and she didn't want Mercy to see.

Mercy felt like crying too.

CHAPTER 17

On Saturday morning, the house was busy.

Mr. de Wet from over the road came with one of his huge sons called Clive. He brought a set of tools and coils of plastic pipe to install a sink that Aunt Mary had bought second hand from Potluck Seconds in Langalibalele Street. And Aunt Flora's old friend Mrs. Mullins arrived early, rolling from side to side up the path carrying two Tupperwares. Mercy opened the lids. Dark brown muffins sat on wax paper with a thick layer of margarine and grated cheese and there were koeksisters: twisted golden pastries dripping with syrup.

"The koeksisters and muffins are for later," said Mrs. Mullins. "But first I need a chair and a glass of water and I want you to sweep the dust off the stoep so I don't get my knitting dirty." From under her massive arm she pulled out a cloth bag from which spilled a lot of pale yellow knitting. Mercy fetched her chair and her water and swept a patch of the stoep. She really wanted to go out back to help clear boxes from the outside room but Mrs. Mullins wanted someone to listen to her while she talked.

As Mrs. Mullins sank into her chair with a sigh, Mercy

hoped the old canvas would hold her great weight. Leaning forward over her knees, Mrs. Mullins used one of her knitting needles to poke the tea bags that lay along the low wall drying in the sun. "Did I ever tell you about the time my brother made biltong out of veld mice?" she asked.

Mercy knew better than to say "yes." When some old people decide to tell you a story, there is nothing that will stop them; they'll tell it again just to check that you remembered it right. So she tried to look interested in Mrs. Mullins' brother and the way he'd skinned and salted the tiny veld mice and pinned them to dry on the woodhouse wall with drawing pins—for the third time.

But when Mercy heard "Help!" from outside the kitchen door, she jumped up and ran around the back of the house where she found Aunt Mary staggering under the weight of a big cardboard box with a rotting bottom, clutching at magazines that were slithering out of her grasp onto the path.

"Good grief!" said Aunt Mary. "There's too much rubbish here to even fit along the passage. I suppose we should sort it before we throw it all out. Some of it can go to Hospice."

"You can put stuff in my room if you want," Mercy offered.

"All right, just pick up these magazines and dump them there," said Aunt Mary. "And then Mercy, please set up the sewing machine on the veranda and sit next to Flora. But for heaven's sake make sure she remembers that she's just shortening curtains and not making a large pleated skirt or something."

She pulled a moldy set of long blue curtains from a box and gave them a shake. Spiders and silverfish fell onto the paving and Lemon darted out from where she'd settled in a dust bowl under the guava tree to peck at them before they could scurry away under the doormat.

"Mary! Mercy! Look what I found behind the geranium bush outside the back room," said Aunt Flora, coming down the path towards them holding out her apron skirt full of eggs. "I have solved the mystery of where...um...that chicken has been laying." She disappeared into the kitchen.

"Most of those eggs will be rotten," said Aunt Mary. "We mustn't let her get hold of them and start making omelettes; they'll stink the house out. Oh good Lord! Mr. de Wet wanted me to cut off the water for him. That sink..."

She disappeared.

Mercy picked up the magazines outside the kitchen and tossed them in her bedroom, then she dragged the old Singer sewing machine on its metal stand out onto the stoep and helped Aunt Flora to pin up the hems.

Mr. de Wet strode up and down the path, shouting over his shoulder to his son as he went, saying things like "Use the big wrench" and "I'm going to buy some more rubber gaskets."

Aunt Mary huffed and puffed behind them in the house, sorting the magazines into piles in the passage and dumping boxes of clutter in Mercy's room. Even Lemon was busy, jerking up and down the passage, jabbing at the fishmoths and spiders and making a happy *krruk, krruk* noise at the back of her throat. But suddenly, *KWAAAAK!*...Aunt Mary must have trodden on Lemon in the darkness of the passage. Mercy shot off her chair, but by the time she got there Aunt Mary had already scooped up the chicken, put her in Mercy's bedroom, and closed the door.

So Mercy went back to her job on the stoep. She had to pass the pins to Aunt Flora who otherwise put them in her mouth and forgot they were there. Aunt Flora worked the treadle and the machine clunkered away while Mercy helped to heave the heavy fabric up and through the sewing foot. When the hems were finished, Aunt Flora heaped the curtains up in her arms and disappeared.

Mrs. Mullins was telling a long and boring story about a recipe: "So I said to Doreen that she should use the casserole with the lid if she didn't want it to dry out, but..." Mrs. Mullins broke off and sniffed the air. "What's that smell?"

A truly horrible smell was coming from the kitchen.

Eggs! Mercy ran through to the kitchen but it was too late. Aunt Flora was stirring a pot of scrambled eggs on the stove and the stink was unbearable.

"Oh my Godfathers! The eggs." Aunt Mary swept in, picked up the pot, and set it on the kitchen step. Then she flung open the kitchen window.

"I thought I'd just get some lunch on," said Aunt Flora, standing in the middle of the kitchen looking as if she was about to cry. "There's not much in the fridge to feed us all, I'm afraid."

It was strange that Aunt Flora was the only one who didn't seem to mind the stink, but Mercy led her out of the kitchen and into the sitting room. Aunt Flora sat at the piano and tapped one key with her finger. *Dling. Dling. Dling.* Mercy felt as if she had a chicken pecking at her head, so she went to help Mrs. Mullins who was flapping an old *Garden and Home* magazine to try and waft the stink out the open window.

And at that moment, Mercy heard someone tapping the knocker at the front door and calling: "Hello. Hello. Anyone at home?"

She looked for Aunt Mary but saw she was outside emptying the smelly pot onto the compost heap with her face screwed up. So Mercy went to the door herself.

"Hello," said a woman, lifting her sunglasses off her head. "I'm Mrs. Naidoo from the Child Welfare. Are you Mercy?" She tilted her head to one side and smiled. "I'm the social worker that's been assigned to your case."

CHAPTER 18

After the social worker left, Mercy sat on her bed hugging her knees to her chest and rocking backwards and forwards. She knew there was a big hole into which children could fall; it was a chasm without end and once you fell into it, you fell forever. She'd teetered on the edge of that pit when her mother died, and then again when she'd gone to stay with Aunty Kathleen and Uncle Clifford. But Aunt Flora and Aunt Mary had reached out their arms and grabbed her back from the brink. Now she knew that once again, she was perched on the lip of that crater.

Mercy had taken Mrs. Naidoo into the sitting room where Aunt Flora sat at the piano still hitting the same note: *dling, dling, dling.* Mrs. Naidoo chose the worst chair to sit on while Mercy went to call Aunt Mary in from the garden.

"Mrs. Naidoo, you caught us at a bad time," Aunt Mary said. "I am so sorry about the smell."

"It's just old eggs," Aunt Flora interrupted. "But not to worry about them, we can give you avocados or lemons if you like."

But Mrs. Naidoo hadn't wanted lemons or avocados.

And she said she was sorry it was a bad time but she had phoned to make the appointment and had been told it would be fine.

Aunt Mary looked at Aunt Flora but she was too busy rolling her apron up from the hem to make eye contact.

Mrs. Naidoo wanted to be taken on a tour of the house.

"I need to ensure that our placement, little Mercy," she turned around and smiled at Mercy, shifting her bottom off the nasty pokey spring in the seat, "is living in a safe and healthy environment with positive support."

Mercy felt Aunt Mary's hand as it gently rubbed her shoulders.

"Of course. What would you like to see?"

"We can start with her school reports."

"Oh, I threw those out," Aunt Mary said. "But you have my word that she's doing very well. We don't set much store by school reports."

"You threw them out! Why?"

"Well, I've always believed that too much praise does as much harm as too little. Mercy's reports are so full of praise and I don't think that serves her well; it's corrupting to a young soul. She needs to learn to do good work for its own sake, not for the sake of flattering comments or high marks. I'm sure you agree, Mrs. Naidoo?"

But Mrs. Naidoo had not agreed. "Please keep all her school records in future—even if you believe they are corrupting to her young soul. I need to see them. I will have to get copies from the school."

"All right. I will. Now let's inspect the house, shall we? It's a bit of a mess, I'm afraid, as we are doing some alterations." Aunt Mary swept Mrs. Naidoo up the passage, while Aunt Flora and Mercy trailed behind them.

Mrs. Naidoo had put her head round the bathroom door. From where Mercy stood in the passage, she could see the bath filled with dirty water and the soaking curtains. Mrs. Naidoo stepped inside as if she didn't want to stand in something nasty, and yanked the old chain above the toilet. But there'd been no water in the cistern.

"We cut the water off, to install a new sink," Aunt Mary explained. Just then the water pipes banged and rattled in the roof and one of the basin taps spat water like a furious cat.

"Ah, back on again." Aunt Mary turned off the tap.

Back out in the passage, Mrs. Naidoo tripped over a pile of magazines that lay in the darkness. She tried to steady herself but shrieked as a spider ran up her leg.

"Is this your bedroom, Mercy?" she asked as she opened the door at the end of the passage. But before Mercy could answer, a furious squawking hen flew right in her face.

Mrs. Naidoo screamed and covered her face with her clipboard. Lemon recovered her dignity more quickly than Mrs. Naidoo and walked in her jerky way down the passage into the kitchen and disappeared.

Aunt Flora clutched at Mercy. "Who is this nervous lady?" she whispered. "Do I know her?"

"May I have a word with you outside?" Mrs. Naidoo asked Aunt Mary.

Mercy crept into Aunt Flora's bedroom to listen as they stood on the stoep talking in low voices. Mrs. Naidoo sat on the low brick wall with her pen poised over the clip board.

"What about her extramural program?" Mrs. Naidoo asked.

"*Extramural* program?" she heard Aunt Mary say.

"Ballet, art classes, piano lessons..."

"I know what extramurals are. I just don't think she needs them. She has a perfectly good *intramural* program at home. Right here, where all the best learning takes place. She can cook, read, raise chickens, play the piano at home, grow lettuces...what more, I ask you, should a child do?"

But then Aunt Flora came and stood beside her, holding out one of Mrs. Mullins' Tupperwares. There was syrup running down Aunt Flora's chin.

"You have to try one of these koeksisters, Mercy. I've already eaten three." But Mercy had no appetite. She heard Aunt Mary say loudly: "Place of safety indeed! *This* is her place of safety!"

Aunt Mary turned and walked back into the house and Mercy ran to find her.

They all stood at the sitting room window. Aunt Mary put her arm around Mercy's shoulders as they watched Mrs. Naidoo walk down the path. She had sat on one of the drying tea bags and it was sticking to her bottom.

"Serves her jolly well right," Aunt Mary said.

CHAPTER 19

After the social worker's visit, Aunt Mary had flapped about the house like a big, angry goose. "Place of safety!" Mercy overheard her muttering to Aunt Flora. "Pah! We'll show her what a place of safety looks like."

So by Wednesday the room was painted white, the sink was installed, and the clean blue curtains were hanging in the window.

Mercy went out early on her bike before school to buy a paper and Aunt Mary spread it on the kitchen table to look for their advertisement. She ran her finger up and down the columns until she reached "Flats to let." It was strange to see the name Mary McKnight and their phone number in such a public place. The phone calls started before Mercy even left for school.

"Hello, this is Mary McKnight speaking.

Yes, the garden cottage.

No, we are not offering day care for toddlers...

No, it would not be suitable as a hair salon, I'm afraid.

Four students, did you say? No, I'm afraid there won't be room.

No, I don't care how small they are."

"Most peculiar," said Aunt Mary. "People don't seem able to read."

Mercy went off to school with her worries like a heavy bag of rocks on her back. She just knew this wasn't going to work out well.

"So who's your role model?" Thando asked outside the classroom as they were hanging up their bags.

"Role model?" Mercy felt the world fall away under her feet. With all the fuss about the lodger and the social worker, she'd forgotten her homework. Her first thought was that maybe she could get Aunt Mary to write a note.

Please excuse Mercy from the oral. She has a heavy heart and cannot participate.

"I forgot," she said.

"You can share mine. I'm doing 'Mike the headless chicken.'"

"A chicken?"

"Mike. Though he was actually a rooster. You can google him. His head was cut off and he lived without his head for one and a half years. In America."

"Without his *head*?"

"Ja, his owner fed him milk and water with an eye-dropper right into his throat. He even gained weight. He used to take him round to fairs and..."

"Thando and Mercy. Sorry to interrupt your conversation with our lesson, but the class is waiting for you. Inside. Now," said Mrs. Pruitt, holding the door open.

After the register had been taken, Mrs. Pruitt called each person's name and wrote down the name of the role model they'd chosen.

"Olive?"

Olive stood up next to her desk and said in a big, clear voice: "The Duchess of Cambridge."

"Good. Nelisiwe?"

"BE-YON-CE," said Nelisiwe also in a big loud voice.

"Right. Yolanda."

"Yolandi Visser."

"Who?" asked Mrs. Pruitt.

"She's a punk singer from Die Antwoord."

Mrs. Pruitt hesitated but wrote it down. She hesitated even longer when JJ told her he was doing Candice Swanepoel, the model. "Are you quite sure about that, JJ?" she asked.

"Yes."

She wrote it down.

"Beatrice."

"Miley Cyrus, Mrs. Pruitt."

"OK. Mercy?"

Mercy didn't say anything.

"Mercy? Do you have a role model?"

"No, Mrs. Pruitt."

"Well, maybe you can do Nelson Mandela then."

Five people's hands shot into the air. "But I'm doing Nelson Mandela!" they all said.

"It's fine. Everyone calm down. The more people who do Nelson Mandela, the better," said Mrs. Pruitt. "Janice?"

But Janice was absent that day.

"Thando?"

"Mike the headless chicken."

Mrs. Pruitt clicked her pen. She waggled it from side to side so that it tapped against her palm. She screwed her mouth to the side of her face and she looked out the window. After a long pause, she sighed and said, "Mike.

The Headless Chicken." And wrote him down.

Everyone laughed and Thando put his hand to his throat and throttled himself.

CHAPTER 20

Aunt Mary was wiping the kitchen counters when Mercy got home from school and Aunt Flora was jamming bunches of leaves and bougainvillea into jugs to fill up the spaces in the sitting room. People were coming to look at the cottage.

When they heard the first knock, Aunt Flora scurried off to the kitchen where she sat at the table pretending to darn school socks. Mercy peeped round the passage wall to see a man with long arms standing at the front door.

"I'm Derek Marshall," he mumbled. He smoothed long strands of beige hair over his bald patch with pale hands.

Aunt Mary took him through the house and out of the kitchen door. Aunt Flora didn't even look up from her sock as they came past and he did not greet her. Mercy trailed behind him looking at the back of his head; it was pink with fine blonde hairs. His grey trousers dragged on the ground so that the hem was frayed and dirty. Something about his sagging trousers, the tender pink skin on his head, and his limp arms made her feel hopeless. He stepped into the room and looked straight at the ceiling.

"How much?" he asked.

"Three and a half thousand a month, lights and water included." He moved the clean, hemmed blue curtains aside to find the plug points.

"I need to put a flat screen TV against this wall," he said.

"Do you have furniture? A bed? A fridge?"

"I don't need a fridge," he said. "I don't cook."

"Ah."

There seemed to be nothing else to say so Mercy followed Aunt Mary and Derek Marshall back through the house to see him out.

"Well, strike *him* off the list," said Aunt Mary as they watched him leave in his beige car. "It makes me want to weep just to look at him. Who's next?" She looked at her list of three names.

Nothing, absolutely nothing on earth, could have prepared them for the second arrival.

A big white van pulled up on the pavement with the name Doctor Waku printed in large leopard skin letters down the side. An enormous man, wearing a long turquoise tunic as big as a tent, slammed the door of the van, strode down the path, and held out his huge paw. He shook hands with Aunt Mary then gripped Mercy's like he was crumpling a leaf.

"Greetings, greetings," he boomed from deep within his chest. "Doctor Waku." The sound of his voice reminded Mercy of the motorbikes that could sometimes be heard on quiet nights growling down Alexandra Street.

Aunt Flora came out of the kitchen clutching the socks to her chest to see where all the noise was coming from.

"May I? Yes?" He pointed inside the house, as if he was in charge. So everyone followed him into the sitting room.

He handed out pamphlets printed on small pieces of pink paper.

I am Doctor Waku, the Doctor of Happiness, from Senegal, Mercy read. *I can solve problems: help you find permanent love, heal general body pains, make your business busy, protect your property or deal with pressure high or low... Due to many customers please make appointments. Phone 092556778.*

Aunt Mary shook her head as if she was trying to shake off some kind of spell.

"If you have many customers, as you say, Doctor Waku, I'm afraid..."

"Madam, I do not want deception," boomed Doctor Waku. "Deception is the source of all troubles and we are having enough troubles in the world. If you cannot accommodate my business, I will look elsewhere."

"We are such a quiet neighborhood..."

"This I can see," said Doctor Waku. "I will continue to search." He waved one huge arm in the general direction of town. "Ladies, thank you warmly for your consideration." He stood up and bowed. "May the ancestors bless you and be favorable. And may there be protection."

And then it was as if a hurricane came and blew him out the door, down the path, and away in his van.

"Good heavens," said Aunt Mary, "at one stage I thought he might turn us all into toads. What did you think of that, Flora?"

"Kwaaak," croaked Aunt Flora. She was still clutching socks but her eyes twinkled as she looked down the road at the disappearing van.

Aunt Mary laughed and Mercy felt a small change in the air around her. Maybe not all of Aunt Flora's roads were as badly damaged as they'd thought.

"Good evening," said a quiet voice from the path. A small

man was silhouetted against the sun so Mercy couldn't see him clearly. Aunt Mary went down the steps to meet him.

"Mr. Singh, we did not see your car arrive," she said.

"It was such a lovely evening, I decided to walk from the taxi rank," he said.

"Miss McKnight, a pleasure to meet you," he said, holding Aunt Mary's and then Aunt Flora's hands in both of his. "And who is this?"

"This is Mercy," said Aunt Mary.

"Mercy," he said, taking her hand. "An excellent name. Do you know what Shakespeare says about you?"

"No."

"The quality of Mercy is not strain'd. It droppeth as the gentle rain from heaven..."

And to Mercy's surprise Aunt Mary and Aunt Flora joined in and all three said together as if they'd rehearsed: *"It is twice blessed: It blesses him that gives and him that takes. 'Tis mightiest in the mightiest."*

"Twice blessed. Yes, indeed," said Mr. Singh. "A virtue only for the mightiest."

Something settled in Mercy's heart. It was as if a chair that had been tilting and wobbling about on three legs finally found its fourth leg and could stand square and solid on the ground once more. Was it his kind eyes? Was it the soft evening light? Was it the poem about mercy dropping like the gentle rain of heaven?

Whatever it was, Mercy knew that they all felt it, because Aunt Mary said, "Would you like to see your cottage?"

CHAPTER 21

Mr. Singh moved in the very next day. So when Mercy got back from school, there was a bright red car with spikey hub caps parked on the pavement and there were three men carrying boxes and ducking under the camel foot tree on their way to the cottage. Mr. Singh followed behind them holding a little tree in a brass pot.

"These are my sons Rajvir, Rahul, and Ramesh," he said. "And this is my tulsi tree."

Mercy said hello to Mr. Singh's sons, and smiled shyly at the tree. Then she went straight inside to peep at their comings and goings from behind the kitchen curtains.

Lemon was having a little dust bath under the guava tree. Mercy watched Mr. Singh put down his tulsi tree and squat down on his haunches. He held out something in his hand and crumbled bits of it onto the grass. Lemon jerked her way over to him and stabbed at what looked like bread crust. Then she ran off with the food in her beak to peck at it in peace.

"Go and invite Mr. Singh to join us for supper," Aunt Mary said when all his sons had left. So Mercy went out to the back room, feeling shy.

The small tree in the brass pot was just inside the porch and there was a garland of leaves and marigolds looped above the door lintel. His door was open and so she tapped softly.

"Come in, Mercy. You are very welcome. "

Mr. Singh was bent over lining up a pair of sandals under the window. The room was very neat. His bed was made; he'd brought a little chest of drawers and he'd made a small kitchen with a hot plate and kettle. A few plates and mugs and a pestle and mortar sat on a bookcase. But her eyes went straight to a tiny table in the corner of the room where it looked as if he'd put a brightly colored toy; a plastic elephant dressed in red silk and surrounded with flowers.

"Come and meet Ganesh."

When she went closer, she saw that it was not exactly an elephant although it had a trunk and large flappy ears; it had the fat tummy of a man, four arms, and it sat cross-legged.

"Ganesh is the remover of obstacles and the god of new beginnings. So I have tried to make him extra welcome and com-*fita*ble today," said Mr. Singh. "I have given him flowers and lit the lamp. We call it doing pratna." He pointed at the red hibiscus flowers and the small dish with a twist of cotton that lay burning at the base of the strange statue.

"Aunt Mary has invited you to have supper with us."

"Thank you. Very kind," said Mr. Singh. "Please tell her I will come chop chop."

Mercy learned a lot about Mr. Singh's family from listening to him answer all Aunt Mary's hundred questions at supper time: he was widowed; his wife Sangita had died ten years ago from cancer and he had lived with his daughter called Deena and her three children in Mountain Rise since then. Mercy felt bombarded by new names. She'd already met Rajvir, Rahul, and Ramesh. And now she had to make space in her head for Kamal, Kumar, Priya, and someone's fiancé called Nalini. The reason Mr. Singh was moving was that one of them (Kamal or Kumar) was about to get married and the family needed the extra bedroom. Somebody was studying dentistry, someone was going to be a chartered accountant, and somebody else was still at school. It was very confusing.

"I think you might miss your family," Aunt Mary said.

"Oh, they will visit. But I am at that stage in my life. We Hindus believe that at a certain age, you retreat to the forest. The cottage is my forest." He smiled. "I must concentrate on spiritual matters now."

"Marvelous," said Aunt Mary as she poured the tea. "I must say I rather like that idea."

Mercy worried that Aunt Mary was thinking it would be nice to retire to a forest as well. But where would that leave her and Aunt Flora?

"And Mercy, tell me how did you come to live in this lovely house?" asked Mr. Singh as he passed round the teacups.

Mercy took a sip of tea and didn't know how to answer. So Aunt Mary answered for her: "Flora knew Mercy's mother Rose and her Aunt Kathleen because they all sang in a choir together."

"I see," said Mr. Singh.

"Mercy's mother died in a car accident when she was just five," continued Aunt Mary. "And then she went to live with her Aunty Kathleen and Uncle Clifford, but that was not a happy time. And then one day Aunty Kathleen asked us if we'd be willing to foster her." Aunt Mary smiled at Mercy. "And we were delighted. After all, it was just the two of us rattling around in this big house like two pebbles in a cup."

"What a blessing for you," said Mr. Singh.

"It was indeed," said Aunt Mary. "And it still is. Where did you work before you retired, Mr. Singh?"

"For thirty years, I worked at Nestle chocolate factory in Victoria Road. But they closed the factory in 2006 and I took early retirement."

"Did you bring us some of that chocolate?" asked Aunt Flora. At the mention of chocolate, her face brightened. She sat at the table folding and unfolding a dishcloth, making it into a tiny square.

"No, I didn't," said Mr. Singh. "But you hit a luck. I have something even better than chocolate...Mercy, on the little table next to my bed, you will find an ice cream container. If you go and fetch it, we can share what's inside."

Mercy was too shy to tell Mr. Singh that she was terrified to run outside in the dark to his cottage. So she flew through the kitchen door, ducked under the guava tree, and slapped on the light in the porch of the cottage.

A stick snapped somewhere in the darkness and she froze. It sounded exactly like a person stepping on a stick.

She waited a few seconds, with her heart beating like a bird in a paper bag, but there was silence. Then the fruit bats started their *pip pip pip* squeaking in the guava tree and she could hear the lilting theme tune of a TV program coming from the house next door. She grabbed the ice cream container and fled back to the main house, banged the scullery door behind her, and smacked on the light in the kitchen.

"Mercy is afraid of the dark," Aunt Flora whispered to Mr. Singh. "That's why she turns on lights and has to have the curtains closed."

"Totally understandable," said Mr. Singh. "I was afraid of the dark at your age too, Mercy. I used to leap from the light switch to the bed in case someone hiding under the bed grabbed my skinny ankles." There was a brief pause. "I'll tell you who else was afraid of the dark: my good old friend Mohandas. But then he was afraid of everything: darkness, thieves, serpents, ghosts. Oh my goodness... the stories I could tell you about Mohandas." He rolled his eyes and looked exasperated. "Unfortunately he was not wonderful at school work either."

"Well, Mercy is very good at school work," said Aunt Flora. "She could read when she was four."

"Yes, I can believe it. That doesn't surprise me. Not at all," said Mr. Singh. "But Mohandas was hopeless. Couldn't do multiplication tables. Struggled with the Gujarati alphabet. Really, he did not show much promise. He used to run to school and get there late and then run home quickly before anyone could tease him. He was very fearful and a very average student."

"I am sorry to hear it," said Aunt Mary.

"I know," sighed Mr. Singh.

"This friend of yours, Mohandas. Is he...could he be who I think he is?" asked Aunt Mary.

Mr. Singh nodded and smiled and tapped the side of his nose. Mercy was confused. Who was this hopeless Mohandas?

But Aunt Flora wasn't interested in the stories at all.

She had opened the ice cream container and discovered that it was full of biscuits.

"You must eat these chana magaj for me, Miss McKnight," said Mr. Singh. "My friend Mrs. Soni made them for me and she uses her special ingredient, condensed milk. I can't eat them because I've got cholesterol." He patted his flat tummy and handed round the golden fudgey-looking biscuits studded with almonds.

Soon Aunt Flora's cheeks were bulging with chana magaj and Mercy saw her tuck one up the sleeve of her cardigan.

Mercy nibbled at a biscuit, but she had no appetite. All she could think about was the sound of that footstep she'd heard in the garden.

CHAPTER 22

When Mercy got up the next morning for school, she peeped through the kitchen window and saw Mr. Singh under the guava tree. He was wearing baggy pajama bottoms and a vest although there was a cold nip in the air. He bent down to touch his toes, leaned backwards, and rolled his shoulders. Then he slapped his chest and swung his arms about like windmills. Lemon was pecking about at his feet.

Maybe they were going to be all right. Maybe with the rent money, they'd be able to buy more food and fix up the house. Maybe Mr. Craven would stop bothering them. Maybe Aunt Mary would be able to pay a lawyer to stop the social worker from taking Mercy away if she returned with a court order. All the way to school, Mercy practiced saying: *According to the Children's Act of 2010 each child has the right to legal representation and I demand that the order be held pending this process.* She especially liked saying, *"I demand that the order be held PENDING THIS PROCESS."* Aunt Mary told her it meant "waiting for a decision."

But as soon as Mercy got to school, she found there were even more things to worry about.

The first thing that happened was that Mrs. Pruitt walked up and down the rows of desks slapping down raffle sheets. The school was raising money to replace the sports equipment and paint the hall and she expected everyone to make a contribution.

"If you don't want to go door to door selling tickets, then I expect you to get your parents to buy at least five tickets on your behalf. Tickets are ten rand each. First prize is two nights for your family at Thala Game Reserve and there will be other mystery prizes as well. We will do the draw at Parents' Evening in two weeks."

Mercy imagined what Aunt Mary would say when asked to pay fifty rand for new sports equipment: "Fifty rand! For *sports* equipment? Don't they have better things to spend our money on?"

"And for the child who sells the most raffle tickets, there will be a further prize." Mrs. Pruitt paused to make it more exciting. "An all-expenses-paid trip to uShaka Marine World in Durban for the day. Now get out your math workbooks please."

And then just as they opened their workbooks, Mrs. Griesel popped her head around the classroom door: "May I have a word with you in my office, Mrs. Pruitt?"

Mercy felt a trap door beneath her feet give a terrifying creak—as if it was about to open suddenly and pitch her into the darkness. It was the social worker. She knew it. Mrs. Naidoo had come to meet with the teachers and she would find out about all the excuse notes and about how Mercy had missed the geography test and sports day and how she'd hardly participated in the class assembly.

"Just get on with those sums quietly, class," said Mrs. Pruitt. "I will be back just now."

Mercy's mouth went dry and although she opened her book and stared at the sums, she couldn't do anything.

When Mrs. Pruitt came back, Mercy expected her to look straight at her with a pitying look. But she didn't. She addressed the whole class.

"I expect you will have noticed," Mrs. Pruitt said, looking off into the distance, "Janice has not been coming to school lately. Did anyone notice?"

Mercy realized that she'd not thought about Janice for days and days. Was she sick? Had she *died*? She turned around to look at the class. Everyone was looking a bit scared of Mrs. Pruitt's very serious tone of voice.

"Well, Janice has left this school. Apparently there were people in this class—and she has not named names—people who were very mean to her and she'd had enough. So she's left and she will not be coming back."

There was silence.

"I think," said Mrs. Pruitt, "we need to have a talk about bullying."

And so they did. Or rather Mrs. Pruitt talked. She gave them a definition of bullying: The use of force, threat, or coercion to abuse, intimidate, or aggressively dominate others. And they learned that bullying takes different forms: emotional, verbal, physical and cyber—which is bullying on the internet. They learned that it is important to develop something called an anti-bullying culture in their class. People who stand by and watch bullying happen without doing anything about it are called bystanders and it's not good to be a bystander. And the best ways to prevent bullying are to:

Stand tall

Make firm eye contact

and

Be assertive

This made no sense to Mercy. Janice stood extremely tall; she towered over everyone. And Olive was all about eye contact. She was always looking at people with her giant magnified eyes. Standing tall and making eye contact didn't help Janice and it wasn't helping Olive. They could try being assertive, but Mercy knew how hard it was to do that when inside you feel small and scared.

"Any questions?" asked Mrs. Pruitt.

But no one had any questions.

"Any thoughts?"

No one said anything.

"Now I want us to put this unhappiness behind us," said Mrs. Pruitt. "And put away your math workbooks. Everybody line up in silence please. We are going to the library to work on our role model projects."

There were now eight people doing Nelson Mandela for their project and there were not enough books to go round. Everyone was grabbing so Mercy stood aside holding her notebook to her chest.

"Nobody is allowed to have more than one Mandela book at a time," shouted Mrs. Pruitt, although there were notices everywhere to say that you had to whisper in the library. "Take notes and then keep the books circulating. You're going to have to share. Some of you may want to consider Archbishop Desmond Tutu."

Then she disappeared into the enclosed computer area to help those who needed the internet, because there were no books on Miley Cyrus, Beyonce, or Mike the Headless Chicken. Mercy was especially relieved that she wasn't working near Olive. She had enough problems of her own without thinking about all the ways in which she'd been behaving like a bystander.

She found a quiet corner away from everyone and pretended to be writing. But really she was just drawing tiny circles. She drew so many circles over and over that she made a hole right through her paper.

CHAPTER 23

"We are outside, Mercy! Out here in the garden!"

And there were all three of them, sitting on the old canvas deck chairs in the late afternoon sun. It was a peaceful scene: doves were cooing; bees were buzzing; Lemon was scratching and pecking and Aunt Flora was slumped in her chair fast asleep. There was a small smoky campfire over near the compost heap and a pot of water on a little metal grid with legs.

"Come and join us," said Aunt Mary who had a pile of mending in her lap. "The electricity has inexplicably gone out, so we are having camping tea. Mr. Singh found us a lovely grid for cooking."

Mr. Singh balanced a chopping board on his knees. He was using the tip of a knife to scrape tiny seeds out of little pods.

"I'm shelling cardamom seeds for Indian tea," said Mr. Singh. "Masala chai. I will give you just so much of tea..." His fingers showed just an inch. "And if you don't like it, no problem."

"What happened to the electricity?"

"I have not the foggiest idea," said Aunt Mary.

"There was just a big enormous BANG!" said Mr. Singh. "When we put the kettle on."

"Mr. de Wet said he'll come and have a look in the morning. So we will have to make do till then."

This was worrying.

Mercy sat cross-legged on the grass and put Lemon into her lap. It felt comforting to stroke her silky feathers. Lemon only had one expression and it never changed, just her one chicken face: beady and blinking. But she did make contented *krrk, krrk, krrk* noises when she was happy.

"How was school, dear child?" asked Aunt Mary. "Bring us the news from the outside world." She licked a piece of cotton, held up a needle against the light, closed one eye and aimed the thread through the needle's eye.

"I have to sell raffle tickets. To raise money for new sports equipment."

"And I will be the first person to buy one of those tickets," said Mr. Singh before Aunt Mary could say a single word. "What will I win?"

"I think it's a family holiday at Thala game reserve."

"Very good. Excellent." He got up to go and make the tea. "We will all of us go."

"Plus I need to find a role model. I have to do an oral— and Mrs. Pruitt has said I must do Nelson Mandela. But there are now eight people doing Nelson Mandela and everyone's taken out the books." Mercy yanked at the grass but it would not come out; it just cut into her fingers.

"Oh, I'm sure between us we can think of someone," said Mr. Singh, squatting by the fire. He was pouring water out of the saucepan into a tin teapot.

"Do a woman," said Aunt Mary. "What about Emily Hobhouse? A wonderful woman who did marvelous things for prisoners during the Boer war."

"Or Fatima Meer," said Mr. Singh over his shoulder. "A great comrade in the struggle against apartheid."

"It's not a role model if I've never even heard of the person." Mercy took a deep breath and puffed the air out so her lips went all rubbery.

"Or there's no need to do it at all," said Aunt Mary. "I'll just tell Mrs. Pruitt that you can't: I'll write her a note and tell her you have a frog in your throat."

"You don't like to do public speaking, Mercy?" asked Mr. Singh.

"No."

"Well, who does?" asked Aunt Mary.

"Oh some people!" said Mr. Singh. "Good golly, you can never get them to shut up. But interestingly, my friend Mohandas who I think I mentioned last night, he didn't like public speaking either." Mr. Singh flapped his hand in front of his face to chase away a bee that was buzzing round him.

"Really?" said Aunt Mary. "One wouldn't have expected that."

"No, he didn't like it at all. When he was a young student in London, he made some friends: a group of people who all liked to eat vegetarian food—as did he. Before he left England to return to India, they had a farewell dinner for him because they had grown very fond of him."

"London? India?" Mercy was surprised. She thought this friend of Mr. Singh's lived here in Pietermaritzburg.

"It's a long story," said Mr. Singh. "But yes, he grew up in India. Anyway when he was in London, Mohandas decided that he would like to say a few amusing words after dinner to thank these new friends. But when he stood up to talk, he could not utter one word. He stood there like a damned silly fish opening and closing his mouth—and at last he was so overcome by his own foolishness that he sat down and someone else had to read the speech for him."

"He must have felt stupid."

"He did. But he got better at it. In fact he said that it was a good thing; it taught him to use fewer words."

"Who is this friend Mohandas? How come you know him too, Aunt Mary?"

Aunt Mary and Mr. Singh smiled at each other as if they had a secret and then Mr. Singh said, "I will take you to meet him. It will be my pleasure."

"Does he live here now? In Pietermaritzburg?"

"Oh you will see, you will see!" said Mr. Singh. "I will take you on Saturday morning. Now I want you to try this masala chai tea." He handed round spiced tea in teacups. "I'm just going to fetch some sugar."

While he was gone, Mercy gave Aunt Mary the notice about Parents' Evening. She had to sign to say that she had read the notice. Mrs. Pruitt had said she was going to check and anyone who didn't hand in a signed slip the next day would get a demerit.

"Number of guests: 2," Aunt Mary wrote in the space provided. And Mercy's heart sank. That meant Aunt Flora would be coming to the Parents' Evening too. Mercy looked at her asleep, collapsed in the deck chair with her thin legs, floppy head, and fluffy white hair. She was wearing slippers and bobbly blue tracksuit pants pulled up to her armpits. When had her legs got so thin? It was impossible to think of Aunt Flora coming to school as anybody's parent.

When Mr. Singh brought out the sugar bowl, Aunt Flora

woke up and looked about her, a bit confused.

"Is it morning already?" she asked. "What am I going to do today?"

"No, my dear," said Aunt Mary, stirring sugar into her tea. "It's four o'clock in the afternoon and Mr. Singh has made you some special spiced tea. Here, drink this."

Aunt Flora took a glass of tea and had a tiny suspicious sip.

"Hmmm," she said and smacked her lips. Then she looked at Aunt Mary through narrowed eyes. "What's in this?"

"Black tea," said Mr. Singh. "Then I add sugar, cardamom, cinnamon, ginger and my special secret ingredients: a tiny pinch of cloves and cumin."

"Clothes and a human?" Aunt Flora screwed up her face as if she'd sucked a lemon.

"Don't be silly," said Aunt Mary. "He said cloves and cumin."

Mercy looked at Mr. Singh. He was chewing the inside of his cheeks trying to keep a straight face, but his eyes were sparkling. Then Aunt Mary started to cackle. Aunt Flora giggled, and Mr. Singh slapped his knees, kicked his feet in the air, and hooted with delight.

And when Mercy laughed, the masala chai came shooting out of her nose all over the information slip with Aunt Mary's signature.

CHAPTER 24

It was a relief for Mercy to get home on Friday afternoon. It was humid and her school shirt was sticking to her back. She went straight to her room, kicked off her hot socks and shoes, and flopped back on her bed, staring at the ceiling.

Something nasty had happened at school that day. After the final bell, she'd gone to the toilet before going to get her bike. She had been trying to avoid Olive ever since they'd had that conversation about her not coming to Mercy's house. Mercy felt that Olive was avoiding her as well. She'd been avoiding everyone. Mercy recognized the look on Olive's face these days: like it was taking all her energy to keep herself together and there was nothing to spare. She'd stopped volunteering to be helpful, spent most of her break time in the library, and never spoke to anyone.

In the girls' toilet, Mercy heard someone come in to the stall next to hers, take toilet paper off the roll, blow her nose, and wash her hands at the basin.

She only realized who it was when she heard "Hi Olive," said in the sing-song voices belonging to Nelisiwe and Beatrice.

Olive mumbled something Mercy couldn't hear because of the whooshing tap.

"Um, Olive," said Beatrice. "If you'd like to come to my party at the Wimpy this coming Friday, it'd be cool."

"Really? Am I invited?" asked Olive.

"Ja, sure. Sorry I didn't invite you before but my mom told me I had to limit numbers. But now it's cool. Six o'clock at the Mall Wimpy."

"OK, thanks."

"So you'll come?"

"Yes, I'll come."

"Cool. You must remember it's a fancy dress though, OK?"

"Oh?"

"Ja, I thought it would be fun to come dressed as South African food—I got the idea from the Parents' Evening thing. So I'm coming as a koeksister. My mom's made me this costume that's like a twisted pastry. It's so cool. And you must come dressed like a frikkadel."

"A frikkadel?"

"Ja, you know, a meatball."

"A frikka*del*? Really?"

"Ja," said Nelisiwe, "I'm coming as a sosatie. I'm going to have this little kebab stick coming out of my head. It'll be hilarious. Other people are coming as samoosas, biltong... stuff like that."

"A frikkadel?" Mercy could hear that Olive had no idea how to dress as a meatball.

Then she heard them all walk out. The door had hissed and closed with a thud.

The toilet was quiet again.

And by the time Mercy had got to her bike, there was no sign of Olive anywhere.

Mercy lay on her back staring at her bedroom ceiling. She knew she'd have to tell Olive that it was rubbish: that there was nothing on the invitation about coming dressed as food. But she dreaded being the bearer of this news.

A loud clap of thunder brought her back suddenly to the present. When she got up to look for Aunt Mary, the rain started. It came suddenly and hard as if someone had tipped a bucket over the house. She'd been so busy worrying about Olive, she hadn't realized how dark it was so she clicked on the light in the passage.

Nothing.

Then she remembered that the lights had gone bang yesterday. Mr. de Wet probably hadn't had time to fix them yet.

She went through the house calling for Aunt Mary. But there was no sign of anyone.

Maybe they were having camping tea again? Mercy could easily imagine Mr. Singh standing outside in the rain, cheerfully holding an umbrella over the camping fire and waiting for the water to boil. She poked her head out the scullery door. Through the curtain of water gushing over the gutters, she could see that there was no fire by the compost heap. And no car in the carport.

This was the first time she'd ever come home from school and found the house empty. It felt weird and she was hungry. There was food in a frying pan on the stove: something brown and lumpy. When she poked it with a spoon, it looked like tea bags. Had Aunt Flora been frying *tea bags*?

It was only when she slipped in the passage and landed in a small puddle that she realized that water was pouring down the walls. The ceiling boards were sagging and dripping. She ran to fetch buckets and pots to catch the drips.

There was a leak in her bedroom as well, which had never happened before. She put a plastic basin next to her bed and listened to the sad *plink plink plink* of drips as she sat cross-legged on her bed, feeling marooned. It was too dark to read, so Mercy reached for her shoebox collection of odd birds and lined them up on the stripes of the candle-wick bedspread. She put them into little family groups: three beaded birds, five wooden, three brass, four felted and two ceramic. Altogether she had seventeen birds.

She waited to be rescued.

When she heard the car come up the driveway, she ran to the kitchen. Aunt Mary and Mr. Singh were practically carrying Aunt Flora through the rain.

"Mercy sweetheart, you must have been so worried about us," said Aunt Mary, helping Aunt Flora through the scullery door that Mercy held open. "What a hullabaloo."

"Indeed an adventure," said Mr. Singh as he puffed down the passage to get dry towels from the linen cup-board. "Good golly," he said when he saw the pots and buckets.

That afternoon Aunt Flora had disappeared while Aunt Mary and Mr. Singh were fixing the washing line that had mysteriously fallen down. They had thought Aunt Flora was in her bedroom but she wasn't.

They'd hunted everywhere for her. Even the man selling newspapers at the corner of St Patrick's Road had left his post to go and search at the Nedbank Plaza. Mr. Singh had combed the streets of Pelham on foot and Aunt Mary had gone in the car to the library in town, the Tatham Art

Gallery, up and down Alexandra road, Chief Albert Luthuli Road, the hospitals, and the police station in Langalibalele Street. But there'd been no sign of her.

"It was like looking for a feather that had been blown away in the wind," said Aunt Mary.

"But here she is," said Mr. Singh, wiping the floor with an old towel. "All safe and sound."

Aunt Flora might have been safe but she did not look "sound." She was pale as a potato and shivering. And thanks to Aunt Mary's rubbing, her hair stood straight up like feathers. She was clutching a parcel.

"Mercy dear, take this parcel and put it somewhere," said Aunt Mary as she tried to take it, but Aunt Flora hugged it tighter to her chest.

"It's for the King," she said and refused to be parted from it.

"We will keep the present safe, Flora. You need dry clothes and bed."

Aunt Mary handed the parcel to Mercy as if it was a precious object, like a baby. Mercy was surprised it was so heavy. She put it on the table in the hall.

While Aunt Mary put Aunt Flora to bed, Mr. Singh told Mercy that, after frantic hours, they had found Aunt Flora at the cricket oval in Alexandra Park. She had told them she was waiting for King George to come past so she could give him a present.

"King George?" asked Mercy. "Who's he?"

It turned out that King George was once, many years ago, the King of England. He and Princess Elizabeth and Princess Margaret had visited Pietermaritzburg in 1947— and Aunt Flora had walked to the cricket oval when she was a little girl to wave flags and sing as he came past.

"When we found her, there she was singing at the top of her voice in the rain. She didn't notice that King George was nowhere to be seen and neither was his welcoming committee. Very happy she was too, for someone who had walked about three kilometers in the terrible heat, carrying a heavy parcel," Mr. Singh said. He laughed. "But we found her and she's safe now. We just have to remember to keep an eye on her more closely. Now what shall we cook for supper?" He rubbed his hands together. "Lucky we got this little gas cooker." He looked in the fridge and emerged holding out a bowl of bones and an old onion. "Soup? Or pancakes?"

Aunt Flora and Mercy had their pancakes with lemon juice and sugar. Aunt Mary and Mr. Singh had theirs with leftover beans.

Aunt Mary took Aunt Flora hers on a tray to eat in bed. They ate by candlelight in the kitchen, listening to the sound of raindrops plinking into the buckets and Aunt Flora's warbling little song that drifted down the passage.

Will ye no' come back again?
Will ye no' come back again?
Better lo'ed ye canna be
Will ye no' come back again?

After supper, while Aunt Mary and Mr. Singh were washing up, Mercy crept to the hall with a candle and undid all the string and layers of newspaper that wrapped the parcel. It was a big bit of cement-colored pottery: a thickly twisted tube decorated with ridges. Mercy thought it looked like a part of something, but she couldn't imagine what it was.

"So you see, Mr. Singh, this is how her life has been," she heard Aunt Mary say from the kitchen.

Mercy put the strange bit of pottery carefully back on the table without making a sound and stood still in the hall to listen. She didn't even swallow in case she missed a word. There was the sound of plates being scraped and water gushing into the sink.

"And it's been a hard life. I can't abandon her now. I just can't bring myself to do it," said Aunt Mary.

There was a long silence and the sound of dishes sliding into the sink.

"No one is talking of abandonment, Miss McKnight..."

"Yes, but I cannot just leave her in one of those homes; it will feel as if I have betrayed her completely. Those places are dreadful institutions of neglect. They won't feed her properly. There's no affection. No one can thrive in those places."

They were silent for a while. Why would Aunt Mary even think of sending her to such a place? Was it because they were so poor? Mercy heard the gasping noise of dishwater being sucked down into the black drain.

"On the other hand, I'm not convinced that this house is still the best place for her. Perhaps she does need more care than we can give her. It's so hard to know."

"Just go and find out, Miss McKnight. That is all you can do for now. And Mercy doesn't even need to know. I will take her to town tomorrow as I promised. I want her to meet Mohandas, and you can go and make your enquiries."

Mercy heard the clink of glasses being put on the shelf and the ribbed glass door sliding shut.

"Well, I will have to do it, I suppose, but it will be with a very heavy heart." Aunt Mary sighed. "Oh my. I never imagined it would come to this."

"I will pray," said Mr. Singh. "For a calm mind and for the kindest and most careful solution."

"Thank you, Mr. Singh. This situation can do with calming. And to make things worse, I had a chat to Mr. de Wet this morning. He had a quick look at the problem with the electricity and he says we have to completely re-wire the house. It hasn't been done since the 1970's and some of the wires are so frayed that it's a wonder the whole place hasn't burnt down. It's going to cost an arm and a leg."

"Oh no no. My son Rajvir has a father-in-law who is an electrician. I will ask him to come and give us a special price. I can help him do the work. It won't cost much. "

"Well, that's something to be grateful for. You don't happen to have a roofing specialist in the family as well, do you? I can't imagine what's happened to the roof suddenly. All these leaks! And everything seems to be falling apart at the same time. I don't understand it. This has always been such a solid little house. Now suddenly we have no lights, the roof is pouring water, the clothesline has fallen down, and Flora's gone completely bananas, if I may say it."

"Of course you may say it. But I think you must go to bed now, Miss McKnight. You've had a difficult day and you must be exhausted. And tomorrow will be difficult too."

"I don't know what I'd have done without you, Mr. Singh." Aunt Mary gave a great sigh. "I bless the day you came to live with us."

Mercy heard the rattle of cutlery and the drawer slide shut.

She tiptoed down the passage to her bedroom before Aunt Mary would find her in the passage.

When Aunt Mary came in later to say goodnight and lay

her hand gently on Mercy's head, Mercy pretended to be asleep. She did not trust herself to look at Aunt Mary's face in case she saw the betrayal in her eyes. Would Aunt Mary see the terror in hers? Surely Aunt Mary would try to find Aunty Kathleen before putting Mercy in a home. Why didn't Aunty Kathleen ever visit, or even phone? Was it because of Uncle Clifford and all the shouting? Had Mercy done something wrong to make him shout so much? To make Aunty Kathleen leave her and never even visit?

The questions went round and round in Mercy's head until she was sucked down into the dark drain of a troubled sleep.

CHAPTER 25

Before they left home the next morning, Mr. Singh went into the garden to pick a small bunch of flowers: some bits of bougainvillea and a few marigolds.

"I like to take Mohandas a small gift when I visit," he said. "He always likes a few garden flowers."

They set off at a brisk clip with Mr. Singh holding the flowers and some empty plastic packets. Mercy was relieved that he didn't ask her to hold the flowers; it was bad enough to be seen trotting beside him all the way into town. And anyway, her heart was so heavy with dread that she could hardly carry herself.

"It's important to *walk* when you visit Mohandas," said Mr. Singh, taking one giant step for every two of hers. "He himself walked everywhere. So it's a mark of respect to walk when you visit him."

What kind of fussy person could Mohandas be, wondered Mercy, to care about how you arrive when you visit him?

They walked up Jesmond Road and turned right into Alexandra Road. What time would Aunt Mary and Aunt Flora be visiting the children's home? They'd have to go past them and left at the intersection with Alexandra Road. The children's home was somewhere at the end of that road. Mercy had been there before because her class had once had an Easter egg drive and taken a whole cardboard box of chocolate eggs to the children in the home. She remembered the noise, the children pushing each other and grabbing the eggs, and then the matron confiscating them. "I'm taking them away until you all learn some manners," she had said. Mercy never forgot the stricken faces of those children as the Easter eggs disappeared. Did they ever get them back? Mercy kept looking behind her hoping to spot the old yellow car. Some taxis came past, but there was no sign of the aunts.

When they'd left home that morning, Aunt Mary had been helping Aunt Flora to get dressed. Aunt Flora hadn't wanted to wear the trousers and blouse that Aunt Mary held out for her; she was insisting on an apron over her nightie and a headscarf tied under her chin.

But Aunt Mary had said: "Oh no. You're coming with me and you can't come if you look like a mad old bat." Mercy wondered if that was what was delaying them.

"Morning. Morning." Mr. Singh greeted everyone who passed them on their way to work. He raised the flowers as if they were a little flag. Mercy looked down at the pavement, watching her feet in their large slipslops. Out of the corner of her eye, she watched Mr. Singh's own thin legs and his enormous white takkies as they slapped the pavement like duck feet.

The walk was hot and long. Every now and then Mr. Singh stopped, handed Mercy the flowers, and, using one packet like a glove, stooped to pick up rubbish: empty cider bottles, crushed Coke cans, cigarette packets, and plastic bread bags that lay wet and smelly on the pavement.

When his packet was full, he dropped it into a big concrete rubbish bin. They crossed Alexandra Road at the robot and turned into College Road. At the café, Mr. Singh stopped.

"You want a min-er-al, Mercy? What flavor?"

"A mineral?"

"A Coke? A Sparletta?"

"Fanta, please." Mercy never had fizzy drinks at home. Aunt Mary believed there was nothing better than "God's Ale"—which was just a fancy name for tap water.

The Fanta was icy cold. Mercy took tiny sips to make it last all the way over the bridge across the Duzi River, up West Street, and into Langalibalele Street. Where were Aunt Mary and Aunt Flora? she wondered. Were they talking to the Matron at the children's home now? Would her suitcase be packed and waiting at the door when she and Mr. Singh returned home?

Langalibalele was a long dull street that seemed to go on forever with funeral parlors, battery centers, cell phone repair shops and debt counselors. Would it ever end?

"Let's catch our breath here, shall we?" said Mr. Singh who was panting a little in the heat. He'd stopped in the shade of an awning outside a shop called Sizwe's Wedding Clothes. The dummies in the shop window stared out at the street with blank faces. The brides wore nylon lacy wedding dresses with huge skirts. One male dummy wore a white tuxedo with a silver cravat.

"Very smart," said Mr. Singh to the shop dummies and he raised his little bunch of flowers. "I hope you'll all be very happy together."

Mercy managed a weak smile.

"You know that when Mohandas left India to study in London, he had almost no money. But he still bought himself a very foolish white suit just like that." Mr. Singh pointed at the groom with his bunch of flowers. "But when he arrived in London off the boat from Bombay wearing it, he realized that everyone in London wore black suits. So he spent a lot more money on a black suit with a waistcoat and top hat. He said that he used to spend hours admiring himself in the mirror and trying to look like an English gentleman." Mr. Singh chuckled to himself. "Mohandas!" He shook his head. "When you see him just now, you will realize how odd that is."

"Why?" asked Mercy. "Doesn't he wear suits anymore?"

"No, he wears hardly anything these days. He's not fussed about clothes."

Mercy was starting to think this man Mohandas sounded rather alarming. She could not understand why Mr. Singh was so fond of him. So far all she knew of him was that he was bad at algebra; he was once afraid of the dark; he spent his money on foolish clothes; and he didn't like public speaking. Why was Mr. Singh prepared to walk kilometers into town to visit him, carrying a bunch of flowers? It made no sense.

"Are we nearly there?" she asked.

"Nearly there. Nearly there," said Mr. Singh as he set off once again. "Just around the corner in Church Street."

There were lots of vendors in this part of town and Mr. Singh steered Mercy through the crowds. Someone carrying a polystyrene tray full of sunglasses lifted out a pair and walked after them calling, "Cheap Raybans! Just fifty rand." A man selling pesticides from a supermarket trolley was shouting through a loud speaker: *"Rrrats! Amagundaan! Cockroach! Ikokoroach!"*

"And here we are!" said Mr. Singh suddenly.

They were opposite the Grand Shoe Store and Absa Bank. He stopped and bowed. "Mohandas, old friend."

Mercy looked up, astonished. Mr. Singh was placing the flowers at the large feet of a statue that stood on a tall plinth.

The writing on the plinth read:

Statue of Hope

Mohandas Karamchand Gandhi

"*Gandhi!* Your friend Mohandas is Gandhi?"

"Yes!" said Mr. Singh, delighted at the joke he had played. He threw up his hands. Mercy was afraid that he might start dancing a little jig in the street. "Yes! All this time I've been talking about Mohandas Gandhi. Some people call him Bapu, which means Father, or Mahatma which means Great Soul. I like to call him Mohandas because it reminds me that he was not born to greatness. He was once just a little boy who stole cigarettes and was scared of the dark; got pushed around at school; and used to run home to try and escape the bullies." Mr. Singh rubbed his hands together, still loving the joke. "But look, he became this magnificent man, beloved by millions."

Mercy looked up at the statue. From where she stood, he still didn't look very much like a magnificent man: his ears stuck out, he was bald, and his legs were stringy as an old rooster's. He was, as Mr. Singh had warned, wearing hardly any clothes: just a loin cloth and sandals. And there was pigeon poo on his head.

"But did you know him?" asked Mercy.

"Oh no, I never met him. He died in 1948 when I was probably about your age. But I still think of him as my friend." Mr. Singh took out his hanky and started rubbing Gandhi's huge toes. "Look what Albert Einstein said here." Mr. Singh read the writing on the plinth out loud. "'Generations to come will scarce believe that such a one as this ever in flesh and blood walked upon this earth.' I remember how it seemed like the whole world went into mourning when he was assassinated. My father kept the newspaper articles and they said about two million people lined the streets to mark their respects at his funeral procession."

He began to arrange the flowers in a circle at the statue's feet, but they fell onto the steps and the *ikokoroach* vendor came to help pick them up. A small group of people stopped to stare at them.

"He's got spectacles too." Mr. Singh smiled up at Gandhi's large head. "But pranksters kept stealing them, so he only gets to wear them for special occasions. Some of us commissioned this statue to mark the centenary of the time he spent a night in Pietermaritzburg in 1893. I wonder what he would think of central Pietermaritzburg now?"

Mr. Singh looked around, beaming at all the vendors and shoppers.

"Mohandas, old friend," he said, patting the statue's toes, "I'm just going to take my young friend Mercy here to see the station where you spent that long cold night in the waiting room. Then we'll be heading home. Keep an eye on things, will you?"

And he set off once more up Church Street without checking that Mercy was following. But in fact she was relieved to keep moving; she'd felt like a fool standing there while Mr. Singh chatted to a statue.

CHAPTER 26

The station was a long way up at the very top of Church Street and Mercy was feeling more and more miserable. She was hot and hungry; her slipslops were rubbing a blister between her toes and she had no reason to believe that the station waiting room would be any more interesting than the statue. In fact, she felt that she'd been tricked. And her heart was still heavy with worry.

"Where I'm taking you now, Mercy, is an important place," said Mr. Singh as they stopped to buy a bunch of bananas from a street vendor.

"Why? What will we see?"

"Nothing! We will see nothing at all. Just an empty space." He waved his arms wide to show just how empty. He laughed but Mercy was in no mood for another of Mr. Singh's jokes.

"But it's an important empty place." Mr. Singh spoke through a big mouthful of banana. "Because it was the place where Gandhi underwent a transformation. When he was an old man and someone asked him what was the most creative experience of his life, you know what he said?" Mr. Singh peeled another banana. "He said it was the night he spent in the waiting room at the Pietermartizburg Station after he'd got chucked off the train."

"Why was he chucked off the train?" Mercy felt that she ought to know, but she didn't. She had heard of Gandhi. She knew he was famous, but in truth she didn't know what he was famous for. Some people, like Einstein or Gandhi, she assumed were just born that way.

"Because he was Indian," said Mr. Singh. "In those days most white people did not want to share train compartments with Indians, black Africans, or people of mixed race. Gandhi insisted that because he had a valid ticket, he should be allowed to travel first class as well. But the train conductor did not think so, so he threw him off the train, right here in Pietermaritzburg."

Mr. Singh tossed his banana peels into a bin as if to demonstrate and took off up Church Street with new energy. Mercy had to run to keep up.

"What was he doing on a train here in South Africa?"

"You remember I told you that he'd studied to be a lawyer in London?"

Mercy nodded.

"Well, he went back to India to work but he was struggling, because he was so shy. So when someone in South Africa needed a lawyer who could speak Guajarati, they sent Gandhi. He was on his way to Pretoria for this case when the train incident took place at our very own station. Ah, there it is." Mr. Singh pointed.

Mercy could see the station up ahead. It sat, solid and respectable, at the top of Church Street, looking down on the ragged and crumbling shops selling hardware, buckets, liquor and cheap clothes. Like many of the Victorian buildings in Pietermaritzburg, it was made from soft red brick and had generous proportions. There was a wide porch with a pretty wrought iron trim, a tower high up on the tiled roof, and two wide doors leading into a hall.

Mercy followed Mr. Singh through one of the doors across the shiny tiled floor into a small room. It was, as Mr. Singh had promised, almost empty: just two old wooden benches and a painting on the wall. The room was quiet and cool as a church.

They stood side by side in silent contemplation in front of the painting: Gandhi looking down, draped in soft, white cloth, wearing small round glasses. He had a little red mark between his eyebrows.

Mr. Singh's knees cracked as he lowered himself onto one of the old benches. "And this place here was where it all started. This was the place where he underwent a profound change that he still remembered years later as a turning point in his life."

Mercy sat beside him and felt the quietness of the room. It was peculiar to think of someone like Gandhi sitting in the exact same place over a hundred years before them.

"Here he sat, just like us," said Mr. Singh, echoing Mercy's thoughts. "Except, unlike us, he was jolly cold— it was a freezing winter night and he was too scared to go and ask the stationmaster for his overcoat that was sitting in his confiscated luggage."

Mercy could imagine herself being too shy to go and ask for her coat but never imagined that grownups would feel too scared to do something like that.

"Was he just wearing that loin cloth, like the statue?"

"No, no, he would have been wearing smart clothes. The loin cloth came later when he went back to India. Gandhi made a decision not to wear what he called 'foreign fineries';

it was his way of showing respect to the poor. He wore that loin cloth and a pair of homemade sandals everywhere, summer and winter, when he met with presidents or world leaders—even when he was invited to have tea with King George of England in Buckingham Palace."

"The same King George that Aunt Flora went to find?"

"Exactly the same!"

"So why did King George invite him to tea?"

"Gandhi was very famous then. After his time in South Africa, he went back home to India where he fought for Indian Independence from British rule. He went to London in 1931 for a very big meeting about letting India be in charge of itself. One day you'll learn about this in school—as well as what he did for Indian people in South Africa."

Mercy was relieved she wouldn't get the whole history lesson now. "Tell me some more stories about him," she asked, swinging her legs on the bench.

Mr. Singh laughed. "There are so many stories, I don't even know where to start." He paused to think. "Here's one: when he went to London to meet King George and all the other important people, he traveled on a big steam ship with his goat. He milked that goat himself on the voyage and he drank the milk."

Mercy laughed.

"And then when he arrived in London, he refused to stay in the smart hotel with other important people; he went to stay in a simple house in a poor part of London. Everywhere he walked, a crowd of children ran after him. He was very fond of those children. On his birthday, they gave him some lovely presents which he always treasured."

"What did they give him?"

"Two woolly sheep, some birthday candles, a tin plate,

a blue pencil and some jelly sweets—if I remember rightly."

Mercy took her slipslops off and bent down to examine the blister between her toes. She raised her bare foot onto the bench where she sat and blew on the raw skin to cool it down. "So what happened to him here? How come he changed that night from being so shy to this famous man?"

"He didn't become famous overnight—and fame was never his intention. And he didn't stop being shy overnight either. But he had a long time to think about himself that night. He was very tempted that night to just leave South Africa and go back to India where he wouldn't have to experience this kind of racist nonsense again—but he decided to do his duty and stay. He decided to face the hardship of prejudice rather than run away from it. In some ways a small thing but it was the first of many, many times in his life when he did that. And by doing that he changed the world."

Mr. Singh was silent for a while as if deep in thought.

"Have you heard of *Satyagraha*?" he asked.

"No. How d'you say it?"

"Satya...gra...ha."

"Sat...ya...gra...ha."

"Yes. It's a Sanskrit word. Most people think it means passive resistance—which is what Gandhi was famous for, but it's actually two words joined together: *satya*, which means truth and *agraha,* which means polite insistence. So really it means the polite insistence of truth. And Gandhi was always very polite, even kind, to his enemies."

Mr. Singh stood up and looked out of the window. He was deep in thought.

"The remarkable thing about him was that he lived without hatred in a world so full of it. He wasn't mean to people, even his enemies, and he had many of those. He quietly and politely pointed out where they were wrong and then—and this is what made him extraordinary—he quietly and politely suffered the consequences when they didn't like it, even if that meant going to jail, doing hard labor with poor rations, or getting beaten up—which happened to him a lot. Sometimes he refused to eat until his demands were met. Once he went without food for twenty-one days and nearly died. People like Martin Luther King and our very own Mandela were both very influenced by this method of resistance. Not everyone gets to spend the night in a freezing cold waiting room, but everyone comes to a point in their life where they have to decide how they are going to deal with injustice."

Mercy sighed. Mr. Singh seemed very moved, but it meant very little to her. All this talk of injustice, poor rations, and suffering just reminded her of her own problems: she could milk a goat from morning till night but Aunt Flora's brain pathways would always remain blocked; she could refuse to wear foreign fineries—if she had any—but she'd still be forced to go to the children's home; she could quietly and politely insist on the truth that they needed more money to fix the roof and the electricity, but who would listen? *Sat-ya-gra-ha* was all very well for Gandhi, but her problems felt much too complicated and impossible.

And to make matters worse, home was still a long walk away. Her blister was really going to hurt, all the way there.

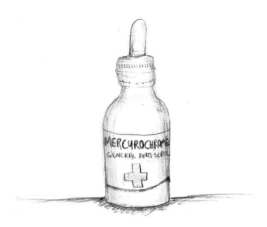

CHAPTER 27

"Gosh, you walked far," said Aunt Mary as she opened the little bottle of mercurochrome and put some onto a piece of toilet paper to dab on Mercy's blister. "No wonder you wore your poor feet down to their nubbinses. Just hold still. This will sting a bit."

Mercy bit down hard on her bottom lip: she didn't want Aunt Mary to know how painful it was. As she hopped down the passage to go and lie on her bed, she heard the slap of the screen door.

"How did you get on?" she heard Mr. Singh ask.

She stopped hopping, leaned against the cool wall, and listened.

"I'm afraid the best thing I can say about it is that it was very clean and tidy and there were lots of rules," said Aunt Mary. "Laminated notices stuck to the walls with the rules: times for lights out, visiting hours, meal times, medication, the usual. It's just so depressing to see them all stuck up there, when it should be like a home."

"Was it not at all homely?" asked Mr. Singh.

"Well, you can bring your own bedding. I saw a few pot plants."

"Oh dear. And what did Miss Flora think?"

"Well. The TV was on and everyone sat glued to it: a cartoon program with a talking pig, if you can believe it. Peppa Pig. Flora was riveted." Aunt Mary sighed. "I had a feeling that everyone was sedated. It probably wasn't just the TV. Everyone seemed so docile. Almost defeated."

"So what did you decide in the end?"

"I filled out the forms." Aunt Mary was quiet for a long time. "I think I don't have much choice. I'm not sure how I'm going to tell Mercy."

"What's the next step?"

"They employ a social worker. She'll be in touch."

Aunt Mary hated social workers. She called them interfering old turnips. But now she was going to get one to actually come to the house!

It sounded as if everything had been decided. Mercy was to go to a home where the only things on the wall were laminated rules. She'd have to watch Peppa Pig on TV with all the other sedated children.

She slid down the wall and sat in the dark of the passage, her head covered with both hands as if the roof was about to come down upon her.

CHAPTER 28

"Mercy? Dear child? Are you all right?" Aunt Mary was standing over her. "Were you listening to all that? Dear oh *dear.*" She reached out her arm, hoisted Mercy up to her feet, and led her to a kitchen chair.

It turned out that it was Aunt Flora who would be going into a home. Not Mercy. While they had been in town visiting Mohandas, Aunt Mary and Aunt Flora had been to inspect an Old Age Home at the bottom end of West Street.

"But can't we look after her here?" Mercy asked, feeling she would cry if she said any more.

"I thought we could, Mercy. But when Flora wandered all the way to the Cricket Pavilion by herself yesterday, I realized that it's going to get harder to take care of her. I have to make sure that she's safe. It breaks my heart to admit it but I can't watch her every minute of the day. After all, I owe her."

Mercy looked up, confused.

"When Flora was nineteen and I was twenty-one, our mother died. Soon after Aunt Flora became engaged to a young man called Skipper Edwards. But just before the wedding, I got sick with scarlet fever, which developed into something worse called rheumatic fever, and my father, worried that I would get heart and kidney problems, persuaded Aunt Flora to delay the wedding and nurse me back to health." Aunt Mary stopped talking and Mercy had a horrible feeling that she was going to cry.

"Which she did," said Aunt Mary, collecting herself. "And thanks to her nursing, I got better and am still as strong as an ox."

"And what happened to Skipper Edwards?"

"Well, this was the sad part. While Flora was nursing me, he took a job up on the mines in Johannesburg. He met another girl and married her and Flora never married after that."

"That is sad."

"Yes. Though she never blamed me, I do feel a debt to her. It's probably why to this day, I have such a horror of making people do things they don't really want to do—like you at school—though I'll never say that aloud to poor Mrs. Pruitt. So now I need to do what's right for Flora—however hard it might be."

Their conversation was interrupted by Aunt Flora, who wandered through the kitchen and out of the scullery door with a basket on her arm.

"Where are you going, Flora dear? It's getting dark and cold outside."

"I'm gathering winter fuel," said Aunt Flora and while Mercy and Aunt Mary watched through the kitchen window, she bent to pick up sticks under the guava tree.

Mercy could hear her singing in a little warbly voice:
Brightly shone the moon that night
Though the frost was cruel
When a poor man came in sight

Gathering winter fuel

Aunt Mary leaned heavily on the sink with her arms and sighed. "Well, all right. If Flora wants to gather winter fuel, then we will help her. The situation calls for courage. Let's make a cheerful blaze in the fireplace and cook jaffles for supper."

"OK," said Mercy, who decided then and there that she would be as brave as possible so as not to add anything to Aunt Mary's burdens. "Jaffles." Although she had no idea what they were.

And so they collected sticks, lit candles, and made the fire. Aunt Mary found the old jaffle iron; Mr. Singh brought curried beans and a small block of cheese and Aunt Mary found bread, butter, and a pot of marmalade. Mercy oiled the jaffle iron—two hinged round metal plates on a long handle—and assembled the sandwiches to be toasted on the fire. They pulled their chairs up close to the fire and ate various combinations of melted cheese, curried beans, and marmalade by its golden light. Aunt Flora insisted on all three ingredients in hers.

"What do you call these things?" She held up a jaffle in one hand.

"Jaffles," said Aunt Mary.

But Aunt Flora forgot the word as soon as it was spoken. "Well, I rather like these gobbles," she said, wiping curried beans and marmalade off her chin.

CHAPTER 29

The next day was Sunday. Mr. Singh was up a ladder trying to clear the gutters of leaves in the front garden and Aunt Mary was cutting back the wisteria that was growing up onto the roof. She and Mr. Singh thought that maybe the reason the roof was leaking was because the gutters were full of leaves so they decided to keep foliage away from the house. Mercy's job was to keep an eye on Aunt Flora who was sweeping the passage wearing a headscarf tied under her chin.

Mercy sat at the kitchen table with an old Encyclopedia Britannica, listening to the *swish wish* sound of the straw broom and trying to read. She'd decided to do her oral on Gandhi. But it was hard. The print was tiny and there was so much information. It was very difficult to work out exactly what Gandhi did and where she should focus. She wished, not for the first time, that they had the Internet instead of just a big old set of encyclopedias. Then she wouldn't have to read all about the Natal Indian Congress; the struggle for Indian Independence; Partition and Independence—things she'd never even heard of. To make it harder, Mrs. Pruitt had said that they had to say clearly why they admired their role model. They weren't allowed to just give the facts of the person's life. Perhaps she could just tell the story about Gandhi milking his goat on the ship and wearing a loin cloth and handmade sandals to have tea with the King of England. But those stories would only make sense if she could explain why he was so famous. Otherwise he was just a nut case who wore funny clothes and drank goat's milk.

Something tickled her leg. She brushed it with her hand and when she brought her hand back up to her book, she saw that there was a bee clinging to her finger. The kitchen was crawling with them: there were bees on the windowsill and all over the floor.

Mercy got up slowly to call Aunt Flora, tiptoeing so as not to step on them.

"Bees?" said Aunt Flora and her eyes sparkled. "Show me."

At the kitchen windowsill, Aunt Flora put out her hands and let them crawl onto her fingers.

"Hello, my lovelies," she said greeting them in her cupped hands. She carried them out into the garden. Mercy noticed one bee on Aunt Flora's chest crawling upwards towards her neck.

A high-pitched buzz could now be heard at the side of the house. And there was a swarm hanging off a lower branch of the pride-of-India-tree, a big bronze ball of buzzing. Aunt Flora gently flapped her hands and the bees flew off.

"Look," she said, "the queen bee will be right in the middle of that swarm. They surround her to protect her and keep her warm. The swarm is nothing to be afraid of, Mercy. It won't hurt you unless..."

"Flora!" Aunt Mary came around the side of the house.

Aunt Flora jumped as if she was guilty of something. "Oh. Oh. Oh." She patted her mouth with her hand and her eyes filled with tears.

A bee had stung her top lip.

"It stung you!" Mercy was shocked.

"That's what bees do," said Aunt Mary.

"I thought Aunt Flora was good with bees. I didn't think they'd *hurt* her."

"Mercy, for heaven's sake!" Aunt Mary moved Aunt Flora's hand away and undid her headscarf to look at the damage. Aunt Flora's lip was swelling quickly and she looked like a strange little beaky bird.

"Ice! Quickly. Oh good Lord!" Aunt Mary slapped her forehead with the flat of her hand when she remembered there was no electricity—so no ice. She hurried Aunt Flora away from the swarm. "Mercy, run over the road to Mr. de Wet and ask him for some ice."

Mercy got through Mr. de Wet's palisade gate using the code she knew and banged till she was afraid the swirly glass on his front door would break. Duke barked like a mad thing from inside and flung himself at the door—but Mr. de Wet didn't come. So she ran next door and pushed the bell that was set into the gatepost on the pavement. No one home there either. She tried two other houses, pushing bells until she was afraid she was going to poke them right through the brickwork, fighting back tears of fear and frustration.

By the time she got home, without the ice, Aunt Mary and Mr. Singh were carrying Aunt Flora to the car. Her whole face was swollen and her head was hanging in a strange way. Was she going to pass out?

"She never used to be allergic," said Aunt Mary, "and she's had more bee stings than you've had hot dinners, Mr. Singh." Mr. Singh got into the back seat with Aunt Flora. Mercy ran inside to get a cushion for her poor puffy head that was flopping about like a softly dying rose on a stalk.

"Can I come too?" she asked, desperate.

But Aunt Mary shook her head. "No dear, I think it's probably best if you stay. I think we...Ah. No, no, you stay here," she said. There was a new confusion in her voice. She reversed fast down the driveway, staring straight ahead of her.

Mercy ran after the car, watching it go down Hodson Road and turn left at the corner. *Aunt Mary probably doesn't want me to be there when Aunt Flora dies.*

She burst into tears.

CHAPTER 30

But Aunt Flora didn't die. She got an injection at the hospital and came home that afternoon with something called an EpiPen in case it happened again.

Mercy helped Aunt Mary to put her to bed, then she made three cups of sweet tea which she took through to the sitting room on a tray. Aunt Mary and Mr. Singh sat slumped in their chairs staring at the floor. Mercy thought it was just the shock of what had happened—but it was worse.

"Mercy dear, come and sit here." Aunt Mary patted the chair next to her and took Mercy's hand. Something in her tone of voice was frightening.

"I'm so sorry about what happened to Aunt Flora." Mercy was fighting back tears.

"That was not your fault, Mercy. Dear child, you're not to blame. The doctor said that sometimes people develop allergies to bee stings quite suddenly having never had much reaction before. No, I want to talk to you about something else. Something I have decided we must do, though it breaks my heart to do it."

"What?" Mercy's heart thumped.

For a long time, Aunt Mary was silent. "I've decided to sell this house and the plot to Mr. Craven. He's offered to buy it off us. And with the money, I can afford to put Flora into a better Frail Care Home, where she can be properly looked after."

"*Sell?* I don't understand. Where will we live? And Mr. Singh? Where will we go?"

"Well, that part is complicated and I haven't worked out all the details yet. But I promise you that you will be taken care of. I have some ideas, but I need time to sort them out. In the meantime, Mr. Singh has offered to have you to stay with his family in Mountain Rise. It won't be for long. Just until I can sort out something more permanent for you and me."

"Will Mr. Singh be moving to Mountain Rise as well?"

"Oh yes," said Mr. Singh. "I will move back home and you will come with me. Temporary. We will all have to just squash up. We can make a little room for you in the garage."

"The garage?"

Mr. Singh nodded. Even he couldn't think of a positive way of saying this.

"And Lemon?"

"Lemon? She comes with us, of course," said Mr. Singh. "We've got a small garden and a peach tree."

Aunt Mary sighed. "If we stay, we have to get the house re-wired and the roof fixed, ceiling boards replaced, and new gutters. Everything is suddenly falling apart—and though I hate to talk about money—I just don't have enough to do all this."

There was nothing to say and nothing to be done. Everyone just sat stunned and shocked.

"I think that this crisis with Flora today brought me

to my senses." Aunt Mary got up heavily from the chair, pushing with both arms. She walked slowly to the hall. Mercy heard the drawer of the desk open and the shuffling of paper. Then tick tick tick...as Aunt Mary dialed the numbers on the phone.

"Hello? Is that Mr. Craven? It's Mary McKnight here..."

Mercy could not listen. She ran down the passage to her bed and lay with her head under the pillow.

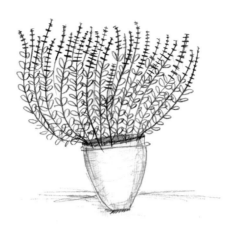

CHAPTER 31

When she got up on Monday morning, Mercy saw Mr. Singh come out of his cottage in his vest and pajama bottoms, carrying a small brass pot of water that he lifted up as an offering before tipping it into his tulsi tree. Mercy knew his morning exercise routine by heart now: he touched his toes, rolled his shoulders, bent backwards, windmilled his arms, and slapped his chest. After that he sat in a chair in the sun, lifted his face and took deep breaths in and out, holding his string of japmala beads. When Mercy had asked him why he did this every morning, he said it helped to calm his mind.

He told her that when Gandhi was a boy, his nurse took him to see the elephants walking through the busy market. Sometimes the elephants would swing their trunks from side to side and steal coconuts and bananas as they walked—which caused a lot of trouble. But then the elephant trainer, or mahout, gave his elephant a stick to hold in his trunk and the elephant walked slowly through the market with his head held high, his trunk wrapped around the stick, and caused no trouble at all. Mr. Singh said that daily prayers and rituals were, for him, like a stick that stopped his mind from causing trouble and stealing bananas.

Maybe, thought Mercy, she needed a prayer to hold onto so she could stop herself from panicking. Did she know any prayers? She started by saying, "Our Father who art in Heaven...." But then she got stuck and all she could remember was: *According to the Children's Act of 2010, each child has the right to legal representation and I demand that the order be held pending this process.*

"Our Father who art in Heaven. Our Father who art in Heaven..." she said over and over.

Mercy had a horrible feeling that prayers would not be enough. She needed something huge and powerful that would swoop down from heaven and sort out this terrible mess. She needed a miracle.

CHAPTER 32

"Oweh!"

Nelisiwe was dancing round the classroom while they waited for Mrs. Pruitt to take the register. She was waving her raffle sheet around her head like a flag.

"I'm going to uShaka Marine World. I'm going to uShaka Marine World..." she sang.

"How many tickets have you sold?" asked Beatrice.

"Twenty. Twen-ty. Just saying," she boasted.

"Oh well, check this out. I've sold thirty-two," said Beatrice wafting her raffle sheet under Nelisiwe's nose.

"Yoh, yoh, yoh! THIRTY-TWO? Don't even lie!"

Olive leaned close to Mercy and whispered: "I've sold forty-three. But don't tell anyone." Olive was looking so much happier. Maybe it was her full raffle sheet; maybe it was the invitation to the party—even though she was still set to go dressed as a frikkadel. Mercy was dreading having to talk to her about that party. There was no way she could do it without Olive knowing that she'd only been invited so that everyone could laugh at her when she arrived dressed as a meatball. How would she tell her?

The problem of the raffle tickets was not going away

either. Although Mercy had decided that she just didn't have the energy to worry about them, Mrs. Pruitt announced that morning that anyone who handed in a raffle sheet with less than five sold tickets would be getting a demerit. Mercy couldn't risk drawing any more attention to herself if the social worker came to school. Surely Mrs. Naidoo was due to arrive any day. Any more "uncooperative acts" and she might start looking again into Mercy's home life and judging that a garage in Mountain Rise, however temporary, was worse than a "place of safety" or a new foster home entirely. Mr. Singh had offered to buy one raffle ticket, but she couldn't ask him for more and she didn't dare ask Aunt Mary.

She was going to have to do the thing she dreaded: go door to door.

Later that day, the class went to the library to work on their orals. Mrs. Pruitt was making a big deal out of this project. They spent all their free time in the library. Mercy was glad there were lots of Gandhi books and she didn't have to fight over Mandela anymore.

She was learning some strange new facts about Gandhi. For example, he had an arranged marriage at thirteen. Thirteen! That was just two years older than Mercy herself. She decided not to mention that in her oral: she could just imagine Beatrice giggling and then asking Mrs. Pruitt, "Is that even like...*legal?*"

She was looking at black and white pictures of Gandhi dressed all in white on something called The Salt March when Olive took the chair next to her. She had a magazine article about the Duchess of Cambridge and she was wondering if she should talk more about the Duchess's charity work or her sense of style.

"I don't know," said Mercy who'd never really thought about the Duchess of Cambridge or her sense of style.

"You see, I think I really like her clothes, but I think Mrs. Pruitt..."

"Olive, there's something I must tell you," Mercy said quickly before her courage left her.

"What?" Olive's eyes looked enormous behind her thick glasses.

"You know Beatrice's party?"

"Yes, I hope you're coming. Are you coming? Because Beatrice said that I have to come dressed as a frikkadel! What are you coming as?"

"Nothing."

Olive looked confused.

"It's not a fancy dress party. There was nothing about that on the invitations."

"But...Beatrice *told* me. She said she'll be coming dressed as a koeksister and Nelisiwe said she's coming as a sosatie...or something."

"No, they're not. It's at the Wimpy. In the mall. No one would go there dressed like that. Like *food*."

Olive stared at Mercy. "But why...? Oh." Her cheeks were flaming.

"I'm sorry," Mercy whispered.

"Books away everyone," called Mrs. Pruitt, clapping her hands. "We have to get back to start cleaning the classroom and putting up the display for Parents' Evening. And save your file on the computer if you are using the Internet."

When Mercy got up to shelve her Gandhi books, she saw Beatrice squatting behind the stacks. If she'd been there while Mercy had been speaking to Olive, she had heard every word.

CHAPTER 33

Friday afternoon came and Mercy could not face going to the party at the Wimpy. It was partly what had happened with Olive and then Beatrice listening in, but also, she only had a home-made present: a paper mache bowl she'd made using what they had at home—flour, water, Vaseline, and old magazines. It looked small, lumpy, and stupid. So Aunt Mary phoned Beatrice's mother and told her that Mercy was feeling *under the weather* and could not attend.

She also still had the raffle tickets to worry about. Mr. Singh had bought one but she needed to sell four more before Parents' Evening the next day. Reluctantly she picked up her raffle sheet and a ballpoint pen and went to try the neighbors.

Mr. de Wet was planting mondi grass on the pavement and he said he would buy one. He slapped himself for money and fished a twenty rand note from a deep pocket in his khaki shorts—but Mercy didn't have change. So he said it was fine, he'd buy two tickets.

"Tell Miss McKnight that I'll come by your house on about Tuesday if that swarm of bees is still there. I said I'll move it for her but I'm just waiting for my son to find the right kit for us."

"OK. Thanks for the raffle tickets, Mr. de Wet."

Mercy tried ringing the bells of two more houses both behind sharp palisade fencing. But no one answered, which was strange for a Friday evening. She remembered that both houses had been empty when she'd been looking for ice last Sunday as well.

"They've moved out," shouted Mr. de Wet. "Sold to some property developer."

Mr. Craven was buying up half the street.

Someone was definitely home at the house on the corner; there was a van parked in the driveway. As she got closer, Mercy was astonished to see that the van had leopard skin letters. Had Doctor Waku moved in? Just as Mercy was about to press the doorbell, the Doctor himself appeared, wearing a navy blue robe that billowed like a thundercloud behind him.

"Greetings. Greetings," he boomed. Mercy had forgotten how deep his voice was. "Can I help you?" He stopped when he recognized her. "You are the little girl. Living with the old ladies." He smiled and wagged his long finger up the road in the direction of their house. "And you are needing help. From me, yes?"

"Yes," Mercy wanted to say. "Yes, I need help in so many ways." But she just asked him to buy a raffle ticket.

"How are the old ladies?" He dug into the pocket of his robe for coins.

"They have to sell the house. Aunt Flora is moving to an Old Age Home and I don't know what's going to happen."

"No. No. But this is terrible. Can I help?"

"Thank you but there's nothing that can be done.

No-one can do anything. It's decided. But thanks for buying the raffle ticket."

"When you need me to help, you know where I am living."

"OK. Thank you."

She walked away but when she turned back she saw him stand with his hand raised like a blessing as she turned into Bissett Road. She wondered about what he said about helping her. Did he know something?

Mercy walked for a while deciding which house to try. Most looked unapproachable behind their vibracrete walls. Some had big dogs that snarled and barked as she walked past and many houses had security spikes or razor wire.

She stopped in front of a big wire gate that was closed with a giant padlock and put out her hand to rattle the gate gently—because there was no doorbell or intercom and no barking dog. And suddenly a memory, one that had been deeply buried for many years, surfaced, like a dead body rising from a bog.

Mercy was tiny, maybe about four years old. She was wearing new clothes that scratched and perhaps it was someone's birthday because she and her mom had a cake. The cake was under a plastic bag and it looked like it was suffocating because the plastic was puffy and there was a knot tied in the top so the cake couldn't breathe. Mom had told Mercy that she must never put a plastic bag on her head so when she looked at this cake, she knew that it was going to die. Mom put the cake on the ground and there was a big wire gate that was closed with a padlock and they could not get into the yard where they needed to take this cake. And then an old lady and Aunty Kathleen came running out of the house with a big bunch of keys. They were scared and they were fumbling with the keys and trying to unlock the padlock but they kept getting in each other's way and looking over their shoulders back at the house. Then the old lady dropped to her knees and reached for Mercy through the wire gate and Mom put Mercy on the ground so the old lady could touch her with her old fingers. The fingers clawed at Mercy's chest and arms and she didn't like it.

Then an old man and Uncle Clifford came running out of the house shouting and waving their arms. And Aunty Kathleen just dropped the keys and stood there and the old lady pulled her fingers back through the wire and her eyes filled with tears.

The old man shouted at Mom and told her something about going home to make a bed and sleep on it—which made no sense to Mercy. Uncle Clifford was breathing very deeply like he'd been running and his hands were opening and closing, opening and closing. "You promised me you'd stay away, Rose," he spat at Mom.

So Mom picked Mercy up and they left the suffocating cake on the pavement and walked back to the taxi rank. Mom hugged her so tightly that she could hardly breathe all the way back to the flat at Nedbank Plaza. And all the way on the taxi, even though she was only four years old, Mercy knew that the reason everyone was so upset had nothing to do with the dying cake under plastic. It had to do with her: Mercy. She was a problem. She made everyone cry. But she didn't understand why.

Mercy unclasped her fingers from the wire gate and sat on the pavement with her feet in the gutter. She closed her eyes. The image of her Uncle Clifford breathing heavily and opening and closing his hands was still vivid in her mind. Why was Uncle Clifford always so angry with her? Aunty Kathleen had loved her, she knew. Her mother had loved her. Why didn't Uncle Clifford? Every memory she had of Uncle Clifford was full of raging and shouting. Was he just angry with Mom for having a baby when she wasn't married? Or was he...? An idea lurched into Mercy's mind like a drunkard crashing into a door. Was Uncle Clifford in fact her *father*? No one ever spoke about Mercy's father to her and she'd never asked. Would Aunt Mary know the answer? Aunty Kathleen would know but Mercy hadn't seen her in six years and had no way of finding her.

Mercy got up off the pavement and walked home. Sometimes the selling of even a single raffle ticket is more work than any person can be expected to do.

CHAPTER 34

It turned out that Mercy did not have to take a picnic to Parents' Evening in an old bread bag as she'd expected. Mr. Singh made the food and packed it in a small stack of silver tins clamped down the side with a clip.

"It's called a tiffin tin and if you take off the lid, like so, you will see there is food in every layer."

It was like unwrapping presents as she lifted the layers of the tiffin tin: roti cut into little wedges at the top; small pea and potato fried patties called aloo ki tikki in the second layer; a red bean curry that Mr. Singh called ramja in the third layer; and chunks of sweet coconut dessert at the bottom.

"Make sure Miss Flora doesn't eat all the dessert," said Mr. Singh. "It's got lots of condensed milk in it and I know she has a sweet tooth."

He'd wrapped plates, forks, and glasses in old newspaper and packed them into a Checkers packet with a flask of mango lassi.

Mercy knew that he'd spent time and effort making the picnic and she knew that she ought to feel so grateful. But her overwhelming feeling was one of shame. They would already look completely different to every other family at Parents' Evening and this food was just going to make them even more peculiar. Everyone else would have cooler bags, not tiffin tins. They'd have steak and boerewors and rolls and tiny carrots and tomatoes that come in plastic bags from Woolworths. They'd cook on skottel braais and drink cooldrink out of cans.

"Thank you so much, Mr. Singh," she said. "This looks really nice."

She helped him to load the folding chairs and a hairy old blanket into the boot of the car while Aunt Mary struggled to get Aunt Flora dressed.

At about four o'clock that afternoon, Aunt Flora had been fast asleep and Mercy hoped with all her heart that she would not wake up in time. But she did wake and dressed herself in tracksuit pants, an old jersey tucked into the waistband, brown lace up shoes and beige socks.

"Why don't you stay at home?" asked Aunt Mary when she saw her. "It's going to be so tiring and..."

"Stay?" said Aunt Flora. "I can't stay. It's Mercy's special school night and I have to be there."

So Aunt Mary took her through to change her clothes and after some time, she appeared, wearing a bright yellow nylon dress with pleats, a brown cardigan with big gold buttons and shoulder pads, and a pair of beige sandals with laces up the sides.

Aunt Flora's yellow dress was awful but Mercy was worried about her own clothes too. She'd tried on everything she owned and her bed was covered in old stretched leggings, shapeless T-shirts, hoodies, and old dresses that Aunt Flora had sewed using the same Butterick pattern over and over. They made her look as if she was about seven years old. The dress she held at arm's length had a bodice, a full skirt, and buttons down the back. Mercy had never seen anyone else wearing anything even remotely like it.

It was easier for her to just go in her school uniform and pretend that she thought that was expected.

She got her raffle sheet and the envelope with forty rand and sat on the front step waiting to go. She took the money out and counted it again: a twenty rand note, a ten rand note, and two five rand coins.

Money. So many of their problems would be solved if they had it. Life felt impossible without it.

Mrs. Pruitt had told them that when they got to school, they were all to go straight to the classroom and hand in their money and raffle sheets. It was already packed with people. Aunt Flora stood at the door blinking. She had taken her cardigan off and was wringing it into a tight sausage.

"Excuse me," said a tall man in a suit as he tried to enter the classroom. Mercy took Aunt Flora's arm to move her aside. The man looked down his nose at them, and must have noticed Aunt Flora's alarming dress.

"Y-ello!" he said looking surprised, then strode into the classroom laughing at his own joke.

Beatrice was behind him snickering through her nose. "Hi Mercy," she said with too much sweetness.

Before Mercy could reply, Beatrice had pushed past her to the display at the back of the classroom. "Hey Dad, come see what we made," she called. But Beatrice's dad took a call on his cell phone and wandered over to the window with his back to the classroom. When Beatrice tugged at his shirt, he flapped her away with his free hand like he was swatting a fly.

Aunt Mary and Aunt Flora gazed long and hard at the odd collection of proudly South African objects that Mrs. Pruitt had assembled. Aunt Flora was very interested in the creepy crawly that Mrs. Pruitt had draped over the back lockers. She crouched down low to examine it and Mercy wondered if she should go and tell her that it was a suction used to clean swimming pools—but she imagined that would only confuse Aunt Flora even more.

Anyone could tell, just by looking at the set of her mouth, what Aunt Mary was thinking. The strange exhibition included a laminated picture of Chris Barnard, the South African doctor who performed the first heart transplant; a Debonairs pizza box; some empty bottles of Appletizer; and a picture of concrete dolosse on the Port Elizabeth beachfront. They looked like a pile of giant knuckle bones holding back the sea. When it was all assembled like this, even Mercy thought it didn't look like much to be proud of.

Not many people noticed the small display of cultural artifacts Mrs. Pruitt had arranged on top of the book cupboard. Mrs. Pruitt had tried to get everyone to contribute but only two people had remembered: Nelisiwe brought a wooden Xhosa pipe decorated with beads and JJ brought a tapestry cushion done by his gran.

"Thank you very much, JJ," she said looking at the cushion over her spectacles. "I'm not sure that a tapestry of a teddy bear wearing a dress done by your gran counts as a cultural item, but beggars can't be choosers. At least you remembered." JJ looked around the class proudly and grinned.

So that morning Mrs. Pruitt had added items of her own to the collection: a small wooden stool with a leather riempie seat which she explained had come from the Boer war and some lace that her grandmother had made during the siege of Mafeking. Mrs. Pruitt loved talking about these items and had spent a whole lesson describing her family history and drawing their attention to the fine riempie work and the lace, until Thando, who was sliding lower and lower in his chair, fell with a crash onto the floor and made everyone laugh. That seemed to shake Mrs. Pruitt off the topic of antique lace.

This evening, though, Mercy thought Mrs. Pruitt looked stressed. She was wearing a new green two piece trouser suit which, if you ignored the bangles and lipstick that went with it, made her look a bit like a grasshopper. She hopped about on her thin legs taking in raffle sheets, shaking parents' hands, counting money, and trying to stop Thando from kicking another of his paper footballs which Mercy guessed was probably his raffle sheet. Mrs. Pruitt couldn't shout at Thando in front of all the parents so she tried to grab him in a jokey way—but Thando just dodged her outstretched arm.

"I'm sorry, Mrs. Pruitt, but I only sold four tickets," said Mercy handing in her raffle sheet. But Mrs. Pruitt had other things to worry about because she said, "Thank you, Mercy," and wrote it down on her paper. There was no mention of a demerit.

"Actually I could do with your help," said Mrs. Pruitt as Mercy turned to go. "If you could count the money as people hand it in, I will write the figures down here and then we'll go a lot faster."

So Mercy sat behind the desk and counted the thick envelopes of money that came in. There was a lot: Olive handed in five hundred and seventy rand; Nelisiwe two hundred and fifty; and Beatrice three hundred and eighty.

Some, like Thando and JJ, handed in only a ten or a twenty. But most people had sold at least ten tickets.

Mercy looked around the classroom, so unfamiliar at night with all the lights on and full of parents. Aunt Flora was back to standing at the door, rolling and unrolling her brown cardigan. At least Aunt Mary was happy, chatting with Thando's mother who looked just like a taller, prettier version of Thando: they had the same smile, the same smooth brown skin, and the same close cropped hairstyle. Mercy liked her blue print dress, hoop earrings, and beads. She saw Olive holding her mother's hand and talking earnestly to her in the corner.

Aunt Mary came to find her behind the desk: "Mercy dear, I can see you have a job to do. Flora and I will get the picnic and go to the playing field. Come and find us when you are finished here."

By the time the classroom had emptied and everyone had gone off to the playing field for the proudly South African picnic, Mercy had counted five thousand seven hundred and thirty rand.

Mrs. Pruitt, full of nervous energy, made a note of the money and stuffed it into a large brown envelope. Then she locked the precious cultural items in the book cupboard. "Oh my goodness," she cried suddenly. "I'm supposed to get the library ready for the junior choir. Thank you for your help, Mercy. You can go and join the others now." She picked up her handbag and left the classroom in a hurry.

Mercy could hear screaming and laughter coming from the playing field and she pictured Aunt Flora and Aunt Mary sitting by themselves on the old folding canvas chairs. She imagined the hairy blanket spread next to them and the tiffin tin. She sat with her elbows on the desk kneading her eyes as if to get rid of the mental picture just by rubbing. She knew she should go to them, but she dreaded walking out onto that field, where everyone else was having fun.

"Mercy, are you still here? Why don't you go and join your friends?" Mrs. Pruitt had come back into the classroom for the library key that hung on a cord behind the classroom door. She had Beatrice in tow and was still in a great hurry. Seeing the envelope of money on the desk, she quickly locked it in the cupboard with the cultural items, then handing the library key to Beatrice, she said, "Just run to the library and unlock for me, please Beatrice." Beatrice took the key and dashed out the room, with Mrs. Pruitt calling after her, "And please return the key! Thank you, Beatrice."

Mercy found Aunt Mary and Aunt Flora in the half light on the playing field. They were sitting with Thando's parents who'd set up a braai to cook their meat. She sat on the hairy blanket and leaned against Aunt Mary's knees. Every now and then, she felt Aunt Mary's hand on her shoulder.

Thando's dad smiled when he passed her a paper plate with a piece of sausage and a bread roll. He squatted down beside the tiffin tin and helped himself to potato patties and ramja curry. "Hmm, hmm, hmm," he said appreciatively when he'd tasted it. *"Mnandi lo."*

Mercy leaned forward and helped herself from the tins. She saw that Thando's Mum used the roti to neatly scoop up the bean curry, so she did the same. Aunt Mary balanced her bendy paper plate on her knees and ate with a knife and fork but Aunt Flora sat with the container of coconut dessert on her lap and, using a fork, helped herself to one piece after another.

After supper Thando tried to teach Mercy to juggle tiny green apples that no one wanted to eat. She darted around chasing a single apple that was somehow always three feet in front of where she thought she'd tossed it. Thando stood in one spot effortlessly rolling three apples from hand to hand in a lovely lazy movement.

"Just keep it loose. Not so tense," he suggested. But Mercy could not master the art.

CHAPTER 35

On Monday morning everyone knew that something was wrong as soon as they saw Mrs. Griesel standing beside Mrs. Pruitt in the classroom; both teachers looked tense and serious as Bibles. The class was so silent that Mercy thought everyone would be able to hear her heart hammering in her chest.

Mrs. Griesel closed the door after Thando had skidded to his desk on the slippery soles of his shoes.

"Good morning, Grade 6."

"Good mor-ning, Mrs. Grie-sel," the class replied in their sing-song way.

"I am sorry to say that we have a serious situation," said Mrs. Griesel. "Money is missing and it's a lot. Five thousand seven hundred and thirty rands to be precise. It was locked in this cupboard." She patted the top of the cupboard. "Mrs. Pruitt returned to this classroom after Parents' Evening on Saturday evening to collect the raffle money and lock it in the school safe—and it was gone. Just gone." She looked round the class at each face. Mercy could hardly bear to meet her gaze. "Does anyone know anything at all about this?"

The class was silent.

"Well, I'll tell you what I'm going to do before we call the police. I'm going to interview each one of you in private. Mrs. Pruitt is going to take you to the library where I understand you all have some work to be getting on with, and I will call you one by one. I want to know all your movements on Saturday evening. Who you sat with or played with and which of the events you attended. We have to get to the bottom of this. Thando, I'll start with you, seeing as you are sitting at the front."

Thando stopped jiggling at the sound of his name and clasped his hands together on his desktop.

"Please get your notebooks and come with me to the library," said Mrs. Pruitt.

Everyone walked out in silence.

Mrs. Pruitt called Mercy aside when they got to the library. They went into the small office where Miss Derby worked. She closed the door and perched on the end of Miss Derby's desk.

"Mercy, I don't believe for one minute that it was you who took the money. But you were sitting in the classroom alone once everyone had left. Can you explain that to me?"

How could Mercy say what had kept her in the classroom? The truth was unthinkable. There was no simple way to tell Mrs. Pruitt.

"I was just...sitting there, Mrs. Pruitt."

"Sitting? But why?"

"I don't know," she whispered.

"You don't know? Well, I suggest you come up with a reason when you speak to Mrs. Griesel because 'I don't know' is going to make you look quite suspicious."

They sat in silence.

"Mercy, I have the feeling that there is something you want to tell me. Am I right?"

Yes, Mrs. Pruitt was right. There was much that Mercy could have told her. She could have mentioned that she wasn't the only one in the classroom unsupervised that evening; Beatrice would have returned to the classroom with the key once she'd unlocked the library.

"No, Mrs. Pruitt," she said.

"OK, Mercy," she sighed. "You get on with your oral and wait for Mrs. Griesel to call you."

Mercy walked back into the library and felt everyone's eyes on her. Although she looked down at the carpet, she sensed the whispering that was going on inside everyone's heads.

At the history section, she stopped at the shelf where the five Gandhi books were kept. As she pulled out a book, she saw a large brown envelope had been wedged upright between them, but she saw it too late and it slid off the shelf with the books and fell onto the carpet.

Mercy stared at the envelope at her feet. Should she bend down and pick it up or just pretend she hadn't seen it?

"Um, Mercy, you dropped something," said Beatrice, who was sitting facing her.

Mercy bent to pick up the envelope and felt the weight of five thousand seven hundred and thirty rands in cash. A shower of five rand coins fell out and landed on her shoes and all over the carpet.

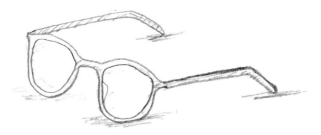

CHAPTER 36

"If Mercy had stolen the money, why in heaven's name would she hide it in a public place like the library and then drop it on the floor in front of the entire class?" asked Aunt Mary. "It's just ludicrous."

"I can't answer that, Miss McKnight," said Mrs. Griesel who was wearing her impatience like a very tight shoe. "We all find the situation very odd."

Aunt Mary had been summoned to a meeting with Mercy and Mrs. Pruitt in Mrs. Griesel's office. As Aunt Mary walked in, Mercy saw that she was still wearing her threadbare house apron over her dress. She must have left home in a hurry. Aunt Mary looked old and burdened—and Mercy was miserable that she was adding more weight to her load. They sat together on a small stiff sofa, Aunt Mary holding Mercy's small hand between her two large dry ones.

"And Mercy seems to be incapable of explaining why she was sitting in the classroom when everyone else was on the field having a picnic..." Mrs. Griesel looked at Mercy who had been silent throughout the meeting.

"Sometimes our motives are not easily explained," said Aunt Mary. "The fact that Mercy does not want to explain herself does not make her guilty of theft."

"No, but a reason would help all of us to understand..."

"Sometimes the heart has its reasons which reason may know nothing of," said Aunt Mary. "I'm sure you know your French philosophers as well as I do, Mrs. Griesel. I think we can both agree that Blaise Pascal expressed a certain truth there."

"Yes, of course," said Mrs. Griesel, though Mercy suspected that Aunt Mary knew her French philosophers a bit better than the school principal. The two women looked at each other.

It was Mrs. Griesel who broke the spell first. "I'm afraid that I've had it in my diary to call the social worker and have her look into Mercy's situation for some time. I've been most remiss in my neglect but I intend to remedy the situation as soon as possible."

"What situation are you referring to exactly?"

"Mercy's lack of involvement."

"Is she doing badly at school? Are her marks poor?"

"Not at all," said Mrs. Pruitt, "Mercy is doing extremely well."

"And the problem is...?" asked Aunt Mary with one eyebrow raised.

"The problem is that sport and drama is part of the school curriculum and Mercy is uncooperative in those areas," said Mrs. Griesel.

"Has it occurred to you, Mrs. Griesel, that some people, who go on to make significant contributions to life, are just not interested in team sports or amateur theatricals? Do you think that Shakespeare would have benefited from being forced to run inter-house cross country? Or that Einstein was impoverished by not being made to sing a solo in the school play?"

"No, Miss McKnight, I do not. But Mercy needs the opportunity to discover her abilities. It is our responsibility to give her those opportunities..."

"If it were just opportunities, I would not mind," said Aunt Mary. "But it is the fact that she is forced to participate and then assessed that I find so troublesome. As Einstein himself once said, 'If you judge a fish by its ability to climb a tree, it will spend its whole life believing it is stupid.' Mercy is a fish who knows her element and it is not the stage. Neither is it sport."

"Mercy is a child who needs to learn to cooperate," said Mrs. Griesel. "She needs to fit into the system."

"Your system is just an elaborate filter to weed out and then punish the children who think for themselves," said Aunt Mary.

It was like watching a tennis match between two players evenly matched: Aunt Mary had French philosophy and wit on her side—but Mrs. Griesel had the weight of the system on hers.

"We should leave this discussion for another day perhaps," said Aunt Mary. "The important thing now is that you have found the missing money. And until you have concrete proof that it was Mercy who 'stole' it,"...she made two sets of inverted commas in the air with her fingers... "I suggest you don't make unfounded allegations. I am taking Mercy home with me now as I think this has been a deeply upsetting morning for her. Good morning to you both."

The wave of Aunt Mary's righteous indignation lifted Mercy up, off the sofa, and out of the door before Mrs. Griesel or Mrs. Pruitt could object.

CHAPTER 37

Mercy was grateful that Aunt Mary did not question her about why she'd lingered in the classroom that evening or who could have hidden the money in the Gandhi section of the library. It was as if those things just didn't interest her. Or maybe she had bigger things to worry about.

The next morning, she overheard Aunt Mary on the phone with the school: "Mercy is feeling delicate and will not be attending school today. Thank you and goodbye." And she put the phone down.

It was, Mercy knew, an important day to be at home: Aunt Flora was moving into the Old Age Home and Mr. de Wet was coming with his son to move the swarm of bees which was still hanging like a big bronze balloon in the pride-of-India-tree. The two events were not unrelated.

Mercy dreaded going back to school after the events of the previous day but what would happen if Mrs. Naidoo came and found her absent? Mercy felt as if the hole she'd been digging for herself at school had got even deeper. Could she ever get out of it?

But the sight of Aunt Flora's small pale blue cardboard suitcase packed and standing by the front door tied up with string made up her mind. The problem with school would have to wait.

Mercy helped Aunt Mary to collect a small pile of thread-bare linen: two lumpy feather pillows, some thin sheets, and a couple of blue wool blankets edged with satin trim. Aunt Mary took down the photo of their parents' wedding and propped it against the suitcase to go.

"Don't make a big fuss about saying goodbye when Flora goes, my dear," Aunt Mary told her. "We will see her every day where she is going and the calmer we are, the more she will trust us."

"Doesn't she need to know what's happening?" Mercy whispered, thinking that if she was the one being taken away, she would rather know.

"Sometimes it is more loving to keep difficult information to yourself," said Aunt Mary. "We have to bear the weight of this for her; she doesn't have the strength."

Mercy worried what other difficult information Aunt Mary might be holding back. Were there things Aunt Mary might think she, Mercy, would not be able to bear?

When Aunt Mary drove off with Aunt Flora, Mercy was not there to watch. She and Mr. Singh had gone next door to the plot to cut away the kikuyu grass that had grown over the old bee hive that stood quietly rotting under the wild pear tree. The hive consisted of two boxes stacked on top of each other: a big brood box at the bottom and a smaller box called a super that sat under the lid. Mr. de Wet was going to move the swarm from the pride-of-India tree into the brood box.

Mr. Singh inspected the boxes by tipping them upside down. The wood had perished on the outside but there were no holes where the bees could escape. He cleaned the boxes with a soft brush while Mercy found four bricks hidden in the long grass. Then they set the brood box right on its new feet and stacked the super above it. Wooden frames that Mr. de Wet had dropped off that morning slotted into the boxes. The frames were to support the honeycomb that the bees would make. Finally they replaced the lid.

They heard the car reversing out of the driveway and Mercy stood on tiptoe to see the old yellow car turn the corner of Hodson Road and disappear. Mr. Singh took off his sunhat and held it in both hands as if they were attending a funeral, which in a way, they were. Mercy fought back tears.

Soon after, Mr. de Wet called them from the fence. "It's safe to start. We better get going."

Mr. de Wet and his son Clive looked like astronauts in their big white overalls, white gloves, white gumboots and hats with veils to protect their faces. Mr. Singh explained that bees are more bothered by dark colors. "If you wear black clothes, they might think you are a honey badger and attack you," he said.

"Can I watch?" asked Mercy.

"OK. But I want you behind a closed window inside the house," said Mr. de Wet. "And you better take that hen with you. You don't want to play silly buggers with a swarm of bees."

Mercy scooped up Lemon and hugged her close. They went into her bedroom and looked out of the window. She stroked Lemon's silky head with one finger while she watched. Mr. Singh stood beside them.

"If you want to capture a swarm, you have to get the

queen bee, Mercy. All the bees follow the queen bee. She'll be right there in the middle."

Mr. de Wet and Clive had positioned a cardboard box on a white sheet under the swarm. Using clippers, they cut through the branch where the bees were hanging and dangled the bee-heavy branch over the box. Mercy held her breath. Clive gave the branch a shake and the ball of bees fell into the box. They closed the flaps and folded the box up into the sheet. Mr. de Wet carried the whole white bundle to the fence and handed it to his son. They disappeared, followed by a few stray bees that had missed the capture.

"Did you know that a single bee working all its life will only make one twelfth of a teaspoon of honey?" said Mr. Singh.

"One twelfth of a teaspoon? That's like...nothing." Mercy thought there was something a bit depressing about that; just the teeniest tip of a teaspoon, for your life's work.

"Well, the tiny drips of honey add up so that eventually you get liters of honey from one hive. And, do you know what would happen if the bees didn't do their work?"

"No honey?"

"Yes, but also no apples, no nuts, no oranges, berries, peaches, avocados or tomatoes either...so much of fruit and vegetables need bees. Because while they are doing this busy work collecting nectar, bees are also doing for the world a great kindness—which is pollination. Do you remember that poem that Shakespeare wrote? About mercy?"

"About the blessing?"

"Yes, mercy blesses him that gives and him that takes. It's the same thing with flowers and bees; give and take. It enriches both. It's a little act of mercy and a miracle. A beautiful arrangement."

Mercy was quiet thinking about that.

"It's in the tiny little circles of life, Mercy, where the sweetness lives. Not always in the big noisy things."

And then, right on cue, there was a big noisy banging on the front door.

BANG! BANG! BANG!

Mercy, Lemon, and Mr. Singh went to investigate and found Mr. Craven leaning his sweaty body against the doorframe as if he already owned the place.

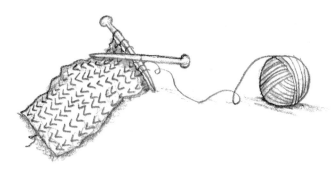

CHAPTER 38

"I am looking for Mrs. Macmuffin," said Mr. Craven. "She at home?"

Mercy noticed the big sweat mark under his armpit once again.

"No," said Mr. Singh. "Mrs. Macmuffin does not live here. But Miss McKnight will be back later. Can I help you?"

"Ja, tell her I came. Tell her she's only supposed to be moving out at the end of the month, but I'm just going to be bringing my chainsaw and a Bobcat in to start work on the trees."

"The trees?"

"We are going to get the bigger trees down so we can get the big grader in at the end of the month to demolish the house. This is just a courtesy, so she doesn't freak out if she sees some trees going down."

"Do you have permission? Before transfer has even gone through?"

"I'll tell you what I have got. I got one helluva busy schedule to stick to. You just tell Mrs. MacFright or whatever the hell her name is. OK?"

"I'll make sure she gets the information, Mr. Brazen."

"It's Craven, not Brazen."

"All right, Mr. Raisin, I will be sure to tell her."

Mr. Craven gave up and with an exasperated wave of his hand he turned and walked down the path.

Mercy didn't know whether to laugh or cry.

"I think I need to let Miss McKnight know what's happening here, Mercy. We may need to get a lawyer. Where's that number for the Old Age Home?"

Mercy opened the desk drawer and rifled through papers for the pamphlet which she passed to Mr. Singh.

He dialed the numbers and looked puzzled. He jiggled the buttons and shook the handset—but there was no dial tone. The phone was dead.

"I'm going to find Mr. de Wet. Maybe we can use his cell phone."

Mr. Singh was gone a long time and Mercy wasn't sure what to do with herself. She was knitting Aunt Flora a hot water bottle cover with scraps of wool so she sat on the veranda trying to concentrate on her stitches. But she dropped one in the second row and when she stuck her thumb in it, she saw it was going to make a hole. She needed Aunt Mary or Mrs. Mullins to fix it. So she just sat and looked at the trees: the pride-of-India with its lovely pink flowers, the camel's foot tree that gave shade to the carport, and the pecan nut tree where the doves liked to roost. She could not imagine them cut down. It was impossible really to imagine such destruction.

Mr. de Wet, still wearing his white overalls, came striding up the path pulling off his gloves. Mr. Singh was trotting to keep up.

Mr. de Wet was angry: "Mr. Singh, excuse my French,

but I smell something bladdy fishy going on here. This house has stood solid for all these years and now this guy comes ...and everything starts going silly buggers. The roof is leaking like a sieve and the electricity just goes off. No, man, I just don't buy it."

"Why don't we get up into the roof and see what's going on?" said Mr. Singh.

"Ja. I should have done it when I came to look at the electricity the other day, but I ran out of time. Mercy, where's the trap door?"

"The trap door?"

"Into the roof. There'll be a little opening in the ceiling somewhere."

Mercy ran to the passage and pointed at the small outline of a trap door that she'd never seen opened in all the six years she'd been living in the house. She was surprised that she even knew it existed. Then she went to help Mr. Singh maneuver the heavy wooden ladder through the front door. It was still propped up against the side of the house from Sunday's gutter cleaning.

She watched the two men heave themselves up into the hole in the ceiling. First Mr. de Wet's big white legs hung down, and, with a lot of huffing and puffing, disappeared from sight. Then Mr. Singh's thin legs dangled down like a mosquito's and disappeared. She stood in the passage looking up into the black hole and heard them thumping and bumping about, their voices muffled.

"Mr. Singh. Check this out!" Mr. de Wet shouted. "Bliksem!" She heard a thud. He must have dropped the torch.

Then Mr. de Wet's big face appeared in the hole.

"Mercy, tell Clive to bring his cell—we got to get some

pictures of this."

Mercy ran across the road. Clive was busy peeling off his bee suit in the back of his bakkie. They returned with the cell phone and he was up the ladder, taking two rungs at a time.

Mercy was once again left at the bottom looking up. She climbed the ladder carefully and stood on tiptoes to see whatever it was that was causing all the excitement. The attic was hot and dark except for the torchlight waving about at the far end. But she could make out the shapes of boxes right near the entrance. The men were coming back, so she scurried back down.

"Definitely signs of tampering," said Mr. de Wet. "That slimy bugger has taken roof tiles off and then *stacked* them. Like we'd be too bladdy stupid to notice. And I can see that he's cut through electrical cable. A clean cut." He held a pair of pliers by one handle with his hanky. "He even left these behind. The chop."

"But how did he get up? Did he break into the house?" Mercy hated to think of sweaty Mr. Craven sneaking down the passage and up through the trap door right outside her bedroom.

"No, you can get in through the roof if you know what you're doing," said Mr. de Wet breathing heavily.

"Are you going to phone Aunt Mary?"

"I already tried to phone her at the Old Age Home from Mr. de Wet's house," said Mr. Singh, "but they said she was having a meeting with the matron and they wouldn't call her to the phone."

"OK, Mr. Singh, you come with me as witness. Clive has to get back to his work. We are going to take these photos and we are going to find a lawyer and we are going to put a stop to this nonsense."

"Will you be all right, Mercy?" asked Mr. Singh. "I think Aunt Mary will be home soon."

Mercy nodded, though there were spiders of panic running up and down her spine. What would she do if Mr. Craven arrived with his chainsaw and started cutting up trees? How would she stop him?

CHAPTER 39

Mercy wandered through the house looking at the rooms. Everything was worn, thin and faded, but it was deeply familiar and safe. Without these bare walls and floors, ragged curtains, and saggy beds, she knew that the world was a cold, harsh place—and that without this threadbare protection, she would not survive.

She decided that if Mr. Craven arrived with his chainsaw and his Bobcat, she wanted to see him with her own eyes. So she took the shoebox of birds from next to her bed, dragged one of the low slung canvas chairs right up to the wall where the tea bags lay drying in the afternoon gloom, and watched the road.

Duke barked from behind the palisade fence. A squadron of hadedas landed on Mr. de Wet's lawn, drilled and snapped at the hard soil with their beaks, and took off on big grey wings screaming at the quiet neighborhood. Lemon scratched through dry leaves and gave herself a dust bath. Cars came and went in the distance. Nothing else happened.

After a while Mercy opened the box and took out the smallest brass bird that Aunt Mary had given her. She built a little house for it using the old dried tea bags and left a wide door for it to escape if it needed to. The house looked like a bomb shelter made from tiny sandbags. The big pottery birds' heads stood guard on either side of the entrance. She laid some of Lemon's white feathers on the floor to make a soft bed for the little brass bird and she hung the wire key ring over one wall so it draped like a tiny wall hanging. The other birds hid behind the tea bag shelter ready to pounce if anyone attacked. She moved them around; some of them were frightened and wanted to hide in pairs but one brave wooden bird stood on a pile of tea bags ready to sound the alarm if she saw anything. All the birds had a different idea about what to do in the event of an attack.

"Fly away," said the glass birds.

"Fight!" said the wooden ones.

"Just lie down and be captured," said the beaded birds. "Then Mr. Craven will feel really bad about what he's doing."

And suddenly without any warning, a flat-bed truck with a Bobcat on the back pulled up on the pavement. Mr. Craven sat inside while another man wearing bright blue overalls slammed the door on the passenger side. Mercy watched as the flatbed tilted and the Bobcat rolled down onto the road. The man in the overalls hopped onto the Bobcat and drove it into the driveway. He swerved the small chunky vehicle left so that it was right in line with the camel's foot tree, reversed, and came forward a few more inches. If he drove another half a meter, the tree would be pushed right over.

Without thinking, Mercy ran and stood between the tree and the big scoop on the Bobcat.

"Hey! Bugger off!" shouted Mr. Craven from the pavement. He was pulling on giant leather gloves. He walked down the driveway waving a big chainsaw. "You are going to get hurt if that tree comes down. Girlie, I'm warning you."

Mercy stood with her arms folded across her chest, to stop her heart from jumping right out of her ribcage.

"I'm telling you. Get out of here," said Mr. Craven. "Dumisani, get that kid out of here."

Dumisani sighed and climbed off the Bobcat. Mr. Craven started up the chainsaw with a terrible roar that split the air. Lemon squawked and flew frantically up into the camel's foot tree.

"No!" shouted Mercy against the enormous noise as the big man came towards her. "I have the right..." Dumisani paused and scrunched up his face as if he was trying to hear what she was saying. He flapped with his right arm behind him to tell Mr. Craven to be quiet. Mr. Craven cut the chainsaw. The silence was sudden and shocking.

"What you say?" asked Dumisani.

"I have the right to..."

"To what?"

Mercy panicked. "I have the right to...to demand that the order be held pending the process," she said in a small voice.

Mr. Craven and Dumisani looked at each other in confusion.

"According to the Children's Act of 2010," Mercy added.

"We don't have time for this kak," said Mr. Craven. "Get out of here."

But words were starting to come back to Mercy. *"All children have the right to a safe, secure, and nurturing family and the right to participate as a member of that family,"* she tried again.

"Ja?" said Mr. Craven. "Well, tell someone who cares.

Dumisani, take this kid—Misery, Messy, or whatever her name is—and lock her in the cab of the truck till we finished here. Jislaaik!" He chucked the truck keys at Dumisani and started up the chainsaw again.

Mercy tried to dodge round the tree as Dumisani lunged at her, but he caught her wrist and yanked her back. Then he picked her up in his powerful arms, slung her over his shoulder, and carried her down the driveway to the truck— as if she was a sack of very small potatoes. Mercy kicked him hard with her feet and hammered his chest, shouting. But the roar of the chainsaw drowned out her protest.

She squirmed with all her might while Dumisani tried to unlock the cab door, but he held her legs in an iron grip. He opened the door, threw her inside, slammed the door shut, and pressed a button on the key ring. She heard the doors lock with a dreadful thud.

She pushed buttons to try and open the windows but they would not yield; neither would the doors. Wasn't there a button you could press to unlock the car? Mercy couldn't see it. Aunt Mary's car had little handles to wind open the windows and actual knobs you could pull up to open the doors but in this truck everything was electronic. Mercy was trapped: forced to watch Mr. Craven reach up and slice through the bottom branches of the camel's foot tree as easily as a knife through noodles. Where was Lemon? Mercy knew she would have panicked at the noise but hoped that she'd found somewhere safe to hide.

Then she saw the hooter. She pushed with all her strength on a small trumpet sign on the steering wheel. BAAAP BAAP BAAP!

Making this noise was all she could do until Aunt Mary, Mr. de Wet, or Mr. Singh returned home. And Mercy had no way of knowing when that would be.

As it turned out, it wasn't Aunt Mary, Mr. Singh, or Mr. de Wet who were summoned by the noise: it was Doctor Waku. Mercy was pushing the hooter and looking so hard at the amputated stumps of the camel's foot tree that she didn't notice him standing at the truck window shielding his eyes to see inside the dark cabin.

She jumped with fright. Then she pointed at Mr. Craven and Dumisani who had stepped back from the tree to see how best to fell the stricken trunk. Doctor Waku appeared to sum up the situation instantly. He strode over to the two men and there was a lot of pointing and waving of arms. Mr. Craven wielded the chainsaw but it was clear that Doctor Waku was the man in charge. After a lot of shouting and pointing, Mr. Craven threw the truck keys at Doctor Waku who pressed a button. Mercy heard the doors unlock.

She climbed out, feeling wobbly and uncertain. Doctor Waku was shouting at the two men with the voice of God.

"You frighten little girls? Hey, hey? *Vous avez le cerveau d'un sandwich au fromage!*" Later Mercy learned that this meant, "You have the brain of a cheese sandwich." He demanded to see written proof that Mr. Craven had the right to cut down trees in the garden. "I want to see *formal administratives*," said Doctor Waku. But Mr. Craven could not produce any paperwork.

"*Non permission*? Then you must go!" said Doctor Waku. With his big hands on their backs, he walked them firmly back to the truck on the pavement.

"I'll be back tomorrow with paperwork!" Mr. Craven shouted through the window as he drove off. "And I can do more damage than just trees." He turned at the top of the cul-de-sac and drove back past the house. He stuck his hand through the window and made a chopping movement in the direction of Doctor Waku. "And you better bring your paperwork too. You bloody foreign nationals causing trouble all over the place. I can make your life hell if I want."

"Ha!" Doctor Waku scoffed and flapped his enormous hand to show he didn't care.

CHAPTER 40

That evening the kitchen was crowded with people: Mercy sat on the draining board, dripping candle wax into saucers onto which she stuck wobbly candles; Aunt Mary filled an oil lamp with paraffin; Mr. Singh handed round samoosas; and Mr. de Wet poured Coke from a two liter bottle into tea cups. Doctor Waku stood by the door in his robe like a huge navy blue watchman.

"Tell us the story again." Aunt Mary was delighted that Mercy had rushed to the defense of the tree.

"It didn't help so much," said Mercy. "I just got chucked into the truck and Mr. Craven cut the branches off anyway."

"On the contrary," said Aunt Mary. "You did what you could with that hooter and the tree is still standing. Thanks to you and Doctor Waku."

"In French we say *Je m'en fouts*," said Doctor Waku. "It means not giving a rat's buttocks when your back is..." He slapped the wall.

"Oh marvelous," said Aunt Mary. "*Je m'en fouts.* I think the word you are looking for is rat's *arse*, Doctor Waku. To not give a rat's *arse* when your back is against the wall. It is a brave art—and exactly the spirit I admire."

Mercy was shocked. She'd never heard Aunt Mary say the word *arse* before. She didn't even say *bum*. The correct word, according to her, was *bottom*.

"I'm sorry Mr. Singh and I were not so successful as you, Mercy," said Mr. de Wet.

Mr. Singh and Mr. de Wet had raced into town to speak to a lawyer. They wanted something called an interdict to halt the sale of the house, because of what they'd found in the roof. But the lawyer would only deal with Aunt Mary as the legal owner of the house. So they had driven to the Old Age Home but by the time they'd found Aunt Mary and got stuck in the traffic coming down Chief Albert Luthuli Road, the lawyer's office was closed.

"I'll go to the lawyer first thing in the morning," said Aunt Mary. "Mr. de Wet, if you could come with me and bring your cellular phone with the photos…I'm afraid I don't know the first thing about these new-fangled phones, so I'm going to need your help. Mercy, you and Mr. Singh had better stay here and try and stop Mr. Craven from doing too much damage before we get back with the interdict. Doctor Waku, maybe you could lend your great strength to the enterprise?"

"Of course. It will be my pleasure to be here," said Doctor Waku.

"No," said Mercy suddenly remembering Mr. Craven's threat. "Mr. Craven said he will check your papers tomorrow. Aunt Mary, he might get into trouble."

"Quite right, Mercy. Doctor Waku, do us all a favor and stay well away. If Mr. Craven calls the police and we all get arrested, you cannot afford to be mixed up in this. They might send you back to Senegal."

"No," said Doctor Waku. "I will be here."

"No, I insist," said Aunt Mary and she said it with such force that it was the end of the matter. Mercy knew that Aunt Mary could stop falling rocks with that certainty, and even a mountainous man like Doctor Waku seemed to know he could not prevail against it.

"Then I will be calling up the ancestors for protection," said Doctor Waku. "This I will be doing while you are speaking to the *avocat*."

"Why will you be talking to an avocado?" Mercy whispered to Aunt Mary.

"I won't be," Aunt Mary chuckled. "But I will be talking to an *avocat*, which is French for lawyer."

Doctor Waku threw back his large head and let out a great boom of laughter. "*Avocat*, avocado. Sometimes it's the same thing."

"And Mercy and I will be here to keep the tide of evil at bay," said Mr. Singh, shaking his skinny arm at the kitchen ceiling.

Mercy saw that it would be as easy for Dumisani to toss Mr. Singh over his shoulder as it was for him to toss her. In fact, she could picture him carrying both of them simultaneously. The truth was they couldn't offer much resistance against Mr. Craven. And he had a chainsaw and a Bobcat. Not giving a rat's arse worked once but Mercy had a feeling that Mr. Craven was going to come prepared for resistance tomorrow.

"Mr. Craven's Bobcat is still here," said Mercy.

"Ha! Just because his Bobcat is still here doesn't mean his Bobcat is still going to work in the morning," said Mr. de Wet with a sly smile. "Mr. Singh? Doctor Waku?" Both men nodded. "Miss McKnight, please borrow me a screwdriver and that paraffin lamp."

"Certainly, Mr. de Wet. In the spirit of *je m'en fouts*, I will get you a whole tool box."

Doctor Waku held the paraffin lamp up while Mr. de Wet tried to get the back panel off so he could fiddle inside the engine. "Damn thing," he said as he strained. "You probably need special tools to get inside this bugger."

Mr. Singh pulled himself up into the cabin and looked around. He flicked a switch up on the right above his head and a light came on in the cabin. "Let's keep it nice and simple," he said. "If this light were to stay on all night, purely by accident, it would be certain to drain the battery."

"Mr. Singh, you're a genius," said Mr. de Wet. "It will buy us some time while he fiddles about with jump cables to get it started."

The light from the cabin cast deep shadows around the Bobcat but as Doctor Waku swung the lantern to go back inside the house, Mercy saw the flash of something white against the chicken wire fence that marked the boundary with their neighbor. It was almost as if her body knew what it was before the message had got to her brain, because she heard herself cry "Lemon!" as she rushed to the fence.

Lemon hung lifeless, her head trapped in the wire mesh.

Aunt Mary gently released her strangled head. She handed Lemon's soft, floppy body to Mercy. Mercy saw just a thin trickle of blood out of Lemon's beak.

"Oh the poor creature," Aunt Mary said. "She must have panicked at the sound of the chainsaw, flown straight at the fence, and somehow strangled herself."

Mercy gently touched her head and stroked her soft feathers. She'd been so alive that morning! How could she be so gone now?

"Oh my dear. I'm so sorry."

"Oh *la poule, la poule*," said Doctor Waku and he put his arm round Mercy's shoulder.

Mercy cradled the hen while silent tears ran down her cheeks.

CHAPTER 41

Mercy must have fallen asleep in Aunt Mary's bed because when she woke in the morning, the first thing she noticed was that the mattress felt different; she felt higher off the ground and the light was a rosy pink filtered through the faded red curtains of Aunt Mary's bedroom. Also her hand resting on the pillow was covered in dirt and her nails were rimmed with black. Then she remembered the night before: how Mr. de Wet had dug a hole under the fig tree and buried Lemon while Aunt Mary had held the paraffin lamp and Mr. Singh had said a prayer.

From the unreal, lead us to the Real,
From darkness lead us to Light,
From death lead us to Immortality
Om Shanthi, Shanthi, Shanthi

She turned her face to the wall. In the background she could hear the clunk of the tin kettle on the primus stove—and Aunt Mary shuffling about the kitchen in her slippers. There was something familiar about this feeling. It reminded her of the time just after her mother died. Everything felt strangely quiet and ordinary when it should have been screaming like a world gone mad. She remembered the way her teacher, who usually shouted at the children, had got down on one knee and had taken Mercy's hands into her own and looked into her face as she told her that her mother had *passed away*. Mercy had not understood the words at all; if her mother had *passed away*, why didn't she just turn around and pass this way? It was the teacher's sudden gentleness that had frightened her more than anything. And later Mercy overheard her Aunty Kathleen saying that Mercy should see her mother's body and she had been terrified. *Just her body? Did that mean she didn't have a head? Did her head fall off in the car accident?* Mercy had sobbed whenever the subject came up and then again when there'd been talk about a headstone in Mountain Rise cemetery. She imagined her mother's head mounted on a stone. It was some years before she'd had the courage to visit the simple grave, holding tightly onto Aunt Mary's hand and read the words on the granite headstone: *In loving memory of Rose Adams. Beloved daughter, sister, mother.*

"Mercy, dear, are you awake?" Aunt Mary put her head round the door and Mercy lifted one hand off her hip to show that she was. Aunt Mary sat on the bed and rubbed her back. "I've boiled some water so you can have a wash. We might as well face this day with clean hands and faces."

It was the blessing of hot water and the laying on of hands that brought out the tears—which can sometimes be the effect of kindness. Aunt Mary sat beside her, her large hands kneading Mercy's shoulder. Many years before, Aunt Mary had told her that when a person dies, it's not a one-off loss: you lose and lose and lose for years after in all kinds of unexpected ways.

Aunt Mary just sat with her and rubbed her back, as if

she was massaging scar tissue. When the tears stopped, Mercy got up, washed in the warm water, and ate a slice of bread and marmite for breakfast. She had to face the day.

After breakfast, Mr. de Wet arrived to go with Aunt Mary to the lawyer. He looked different. He'd swapped his khaki shorts for a tight grey suit done up with a single straining button and he'd slicked his hair to the side. Mercy noticed the contour lines made by his comb.

"Might as well dress up for the occasion," said Mr. de Wet as he adjusted a large tartan tie.

"Quite right," said Aunt Mary. "As Mark Twain said, 'Clothes make the man. Naked people have little or no influence on society.'" She took off her glasses, puffed on the lenses: hah! hah! and rubbed them clean with a hanky which she tucked into her handbag. "And today, Mr. de Wet, we need influence."

Mercy and Mr. Singh watched them drive off in the old car. They looked at the garden from the stoep. It was strewn with branches from the camel foot tree and had an injured look, like a person with a bandage around her head.

"Right," said Mr. Singh. "It's just you and me, Mercy." He rubbed his hands together and bent and straightened his knees as if limbering up for the fight to come. "You have already demonstrated courage yesterday so you have had some practice."

Mercy hadn't told anyone what had really happened the day before. She knew, from reading the books in the library, that real passive resistance or *satyagraha* meant not fighting back; you were not supposed to kick a person and pummel him with your fists while you are being carried away. She wasn't sure she could quietly and politely accept

whatever happened—like Gandhi had done. And now Mr.
Singh would be watching. When she'd resisted Mr. Craven
the day before, she hadn't thought about *satyagraha*. She'd
just done what felt natural.

And today she felt tired. All the crying had drained her
and she knew she didn't have the strength for another
standoff with Mr. Craven. Anyway, what use would it be?
They might be able to save the house from being destroyed
and persuade Mr. Craven to reverse the sale—but their
problems would remain: Aunt Flora would still be sick; she'd
still be living in the Old Age Home; and they would still
be so poor. Lemon would still be dead. Saving the house
wasn't going to solve very much.

"Mr. Craven will probably just pick us both up this time
and lock us in the truck," she said. "What are we going to
do after that?"

"Yes," said Mr. Singh, "he might do that again." He
laughed merrily as he hopped up onto the low wall of the
stoep, to get a better view of the road. "The thing is, Mercy,
we never know what's going to happen. So all we can do
is the job that is in front of us. When we've done that, the
world will be just a tiny bit different."

"Like the tip of a teaspoon?"

"Exactly! You're very smart at making links between
things, Mercy." He brought both his index fingers to touch.
"A tip of a teaspoon is all it takes."

But Mercy did not agree. The situation needed a big fat
miracle, not the tiny tip of a teaspoon of change.

"Because after that tiny tip of a teaspoon, there will
be something else to do," said Mr. Singh, warming to
the theme. "Another tiny teaspoon of work. If we do that
enough times, we look up and find...oh good golly! We are

in a new and unexpected place."

Mercy hoped that the unexpected place would not be the inside of a jail cell or a dormitory in a home for delinquent children. She sighed and scanned the road, wishing it would all be over.

"You think Gandhi had a grand plan when he sat in the dark waiting room that night? Do you think he sat there thinking he would start the Natal Indian Congress? Have tea with the King of England? Free India from British rule? He didn't have a clue. He just did the job that was directly in front of him."

"What was that?"

"He needed to get to Pretoria for that court case. So in the morning he bought another first class ticket and caught another train."

"And then?"

"Well, the station master did not want to sell him that first class ticket, but Gandhi stood firm and insisted. Eventually he got it. Then he got his ears boxed by the driver of a stagecoach because he refused to sit where the driver wanted him to sit. And after he got to Pretoria, there were many other challenges he faced." Mr. Singh made step movements with his hands to show how the difficulties mounted up. "And so you see, it wasn't a straight path to glory for him. And it won't be for us."

It all sounded very tiring.

"And who do we have here? Is this Mr. Craven with his paperwork?"

A car had pulled up on the pavement. But it was not Mr. Craven. It was Aunt Flora's friend Mrs. Mullins who Mercy had not seen since the day Aunt Flora had tried to make lunch with rotten eggs. She lumbered out of the car, carrying a large biscuit tin and a handbag.

"Mr. de Wet phoned and told me about your woes," she called from the street. "I've come to lend moral support."

"Come and join us," said Mr. Singh. "We are very pleased to see you."

Mercy ran down the steps to help her. She took the biscuit tin and was glad that it felt so heavy. Mrs. Mullins puffed up the steps, complaining about her back.

"I made rock cakes," she said. "If all else fails, we can throw them at the invaders."

Mercy took the tin inside to the kitchen and poured herself a glass of water at the sink. From the kitchen window, she could see Lemon's bare grave under the guava tree.

Her shoebox of birds was sitting on the kitchen table. Someone must have fetched the birds off the stoep wall last night, where she'd been playing with them when Mr. Craven had arrived. She took off the lid. Which bird should go on the grave? The two large ceramic birds' heads—the ones that had been lids on Aunt Mary's father's tobacco jars—looked the strongest, the most likely to survive a life outdoors.

Mercy put the two birds' heads side by side at the top of the grave to stand guard. Then she found an empty jam jar in the scullery and picked petria and bougainvillea to put in it. When Mr. Singh did pratna, he put small offerings of food on a tiny dish, so she found a crust of bread and some dried mealie pips and arranged them in the scoop of a leaf.

These small acts of going in and out of the house, picking flowers, looking for tiny scraps of food, and decorating Lemon's grave made her feel a bit calmer.

She stood in the hallway listening to Mr. Singh and Mrs. Mullins discussing the trees that were likely to be cut down and what they planned to do.

"Can't we chain ourselves to the trees?" asked Mrs. Mullins.

"We'd need a very long length of chain and a good padlock," said Mr. Singh, "neither of which we have. And it's not comfortable if you have to stand against the tree for a very long time with a chain around you. Plus you have a bad back."

Mercy looked at them silhouetted in the morning sun. Mr. Craven could, with a lot of effort, deal with all three of them. Then he'd be free to destroy whatever he wanted—once he got the Bobcat working. And although saving the house wasn't going to solve everything, Mercy saw that if Mr. Craven did demolish the house, she would definitely be moving to a garage in Mountain Rise. And if the social worker heard about that...She could hardly bear to finish the thought. If they were really going to protect the trees and the house that day, they were going to need more resistance than the three of them could provide. How would she do it? The situation needed a miracle—not passive resistance.

She thought about what Mr. Singh had said about Gandhi and *satyagraha*. Turning themselves passively over to the authorities wasn't going to work here: there was no way someone like Mr. Craven would be shamed into doing good if they stood by politely and let him get on with it. Surely there was something else she could do! Three people were not enough to stop Mr. Craven. She remembered Mr. Singh's words: *"Satyagraha means the quiet insistence of truth."* How on earth could telling the truth help this situation? Mercy felt like the answer was there just on the edges of her vision, but it was as if it was too blurry to read. Why couldn't she see...?

And then, quietly and politely—it came to her.

"I'll be back," she said to Mr. Singh and Mrs. Mullins. "I'm going to school."

CHAPTER 42

When she got to school, Mercy realized that she had no clue how she was going to see her idea through. She almost turned back. But then she remembered: all she had to do was the job that was directly in front of her. And that job was to find Mrs. Pruitt.

So she found her in the corridor outside the staffroom on her way to take the class register.

"Mrs. Pruitt." Her heart was hammering. "May I speak to you?"

Mrs. Pruitt ushered Mercy into an empty office. "I've been worried about you," she said. "After that episode with the money. Are you all right?"

Something had changed in Mercy. After a lifetime of looking at the floor or saying, "I'm fine," "It's OK," and "I don't know," to teachers, she knew she had to try something new.

"No," she said in a small voice. "Not really."

"I owe you an apology," said Mrs. Pruitt. "I have been thinking about that evening in the classroom and I remember now that you were not the only person there on your own. Beatrice must have gone back there to return the key.

I'd completely forgotten about that. Do you think *Beatrice* could have taken the money? And then hidden it in the Gandhi section to make it look as if you had done it?"

The business of who had taken the money was not something Mercy wanted to discuss with Mrs. Pruitt. Not today. She gave a small shrug.

"All right," said Mrs. Pruitt with a sigh. "I get the feeling though that there are things going on among you and your classmates that I have missed. And I'm sorry about that."

It had never occurred to Mercy that the complicated relationships among her classmates were Mrs. Pruitt's responsibility.

"If you don't want to talk about the money incident, there must be something else on your mind. What's the problem?" said Mrs. Pruitt.

"There is a man called Mr. Craven," Mercy began, unsure how she was going to continue: why did telling the truth have to feel so complicated? Mrs. Pruitt nodded, willing her to keep talking. So Mercy decided to start with what was happening now and just let it spool backwards. Her mouth felt dry and she had to swallow in inconvenient places. She looked at the floor while she spoke.

"He's coming today with a chainsaw and he's going to start cutting up the trees in our garden. We want to stop him but there is only me and Mr. Singh and Mrs. Mullins at home and Mrs. Mullins has a bad back. I think Mr. Craven is going to pick us all up and lock us in his truck."

Mrs. Pruitt crossed her arms and leaned forward with her brow furrowed, trying to make sense of this information.

"Let me understand this. Someone called Mr. Craven is going to lock you in a truck? Because you want to stop him cutting down some trees in your garden?"

Mercy nodded. "He already locked me in the truck yesterday."

"OK. And er...where...where are your foster mothers? The Miss McKnights?"

"Yesterday Aunt Flora moved out into an Old Age Home because she's...she has Alzheimer's and we can't take care of her anymore. And because Aunt Mary has sold the house to Mr. Craven. But today Aunt Mary has gone to the lawyer to get an interdict to stop the sale of the house."

"An interdict?" Mrs. Pruitt was looking more and more surprised. Perhaps because she'd never heard Mercy use so many words or perhaps it was that she knew such big words. "Why?"

"Because our neighbor Mr. de Wet discovered yesterday that Mr. Craven had fiddled with the roof and the electricity to force Aunt Mary to sell. Mr. de Wet took photos of the damage Mr. Craven did. But if they can't stop the sale of the house, I'm going to have to move into a garage in Mountain Rise with Mr. Singh until Aunt Mary makes a plan. Or until the social worker finds out and takes me away to live with someone else or maybe even a children's home."

Mrs. Pruitt shook her head, but Mercy kept talking. The stories started out like a thin brown trickle—like water that has been too long in the pipes. They jerked and spluttered and finally they gushed out in a steady stream. She told Mrs. Pruitt how she was afraid of the social worker; how she dreaded being placed with another family. She told her about Aunt Flora's sickness and about how poor they were; about renting the back room out to Mr. Singh; about Aunt Flora moving out and about the death of Lemon.

Mrs. Pruitt said: "Gosh. What a story! I will talk to Mrs. Griesel about what to tell the social worker when she comes, Mercy. As far as I know, she's not come to school yet. We will do all we can to prevent social services from removing you from the care of your aunts." She paused. "I noticed that one of your aunts didn't look quite...well... on the night of the Parents' Evening. Is that Aunt Flora?"

"Yes."

"And...forgive me for asking, but was that maybe part of the reason that you didn't want to join everyone on the field that night?"

This was the moment of truth that Mercy dreaded. She felt her eyes brimming with tears. As she nodded her head, one fat tear fell down her cheek. She wiped it away with the back of her hand.

"Did you feel that you were different from everyone else?"

She looked at the floor and nodded her head again. Another big tear plopped onto her lap.

"It was that," she said thickly through her tears, "but also we had our picnic packed in a tiffin tin."

Mrs. Pruitt looked mystified.

"Everyone else had cooler boxes, Woolworths salad, and braai meat." Mercy gave a small snotty laugh at how silly it sounded and Mrs. Pruitt handed her a tissue and smiled at her.

"I understand," she said. "No one likes to feel different. But you know what this tells me, Mercy?"

Mercy shook her head.

"It tells me that you are telling the truth. You know how people say 'Just tell the truth' as if it were so simple? Well, real truth is seldom pure and almost never simple. But when you tell it and it's complicated, awkward, even embarrassing, something magical happens. It feels *right*. In *here*."

Mrs. Pruitt stabbed her chest twice for emphasis. "It takes courage to tell it and such courage deserves to be rewarded. So how can I help you with your problem today?"

So Mercy told her.

"My goodness," said Mrs. Pruitt with wide eyes. "I don't know if I will be allowed to do that. I wonder..." She massaged her chin and looked up as if she was thinking hard about something.

Suddenly she smiled. "I think there's a way. But first I want to tell you something." She paused.

"The truth—pure and simple," she laughed, "is that I have been a dreadful teacher."

"Not *dreadful*."

"Maybe 'dreadful' is overstating it—but I just don't seem to have the knack. I've tried but..." She threw up her hands. "So yesterday I gave in my resignation. I'm going to be leaving at the end of term to do what I have always wanted—open an antique shop in Victoria Road and sell bric a brac and antique furniture. I know where I am with a cottage dresser and a high backed chair and I'm absolutely brilliant with a piece of Victorian pottery—but I'm not, it seems, so good with children." She sighed.

"I'm sorry, Mrs. Pruitt," said Mercy, feeling somehow responsible. It had never occurred to her that grownups would prefer to do one thing rather than another. Or that they might be bad at something.

"No, don't you be sorry. I'm the one who has let you down, Mercy, and probably a few others in the class as well, like poor Janice. But..." Mrs. Pruitt clapped her hands together and clutched them to her chest. "All is not lost." She beamed at Mercy. "I am determined that I will do one last thing of value before I leave. I can't teach for peanuts but I might as well end triumphantly. In fact maybe, just maybe..." Mrs. Pruitt hopped off the corner of the desk where she'd been perched. She rummaged in her basket and pulled out a fat ring-bound document. She slapped it on the desk and bent over the pages, licked her finger, and turned the pages furiously.

"Life skills...life skills," she muttered. "Ah, here we go. I have to teach lessons that *promote moral uprightness, honesty, and responsible citizenship.* That might cover us. But there is always *Finds ways to address discrimination, promote respect, and equality.* So if anyone challenges me, I'll tell them I'm finding ways to 'address discrimination' and promote respect. I've been wanting to throw this curriculum document at someone for years and now my time has come. I think we can do this, Mercy. And if I get sacked, I'll just be opening that antique shop earlier than expected. That won't be the end of the world."

"What happens if no one wants to...?"

"I'll tell them that it's part of their responsible citizenship curriculum and if they still don't want to, I'll have a private word with Beatrice. I think I have information that will persuade her. And if she comes, others will be right in her wake."

"It's true," said Mercy. "If you move the queen bee, the swarm will follow."

Mrs. Pruitt looked at Mercy with new respect. "Mercy Adams. I think there's more to you than meets the eye," she said.

CHAPTER 43

And so it was that Mercy rode her bicycle home bumpity bump over the grass verges and along the pavements—and was followed by Mrs. Pruitt driving the school kombi packed with some of Mercy's classmates. Mrs. Pruitt had made participation in this act of "responsible citizenship" voluntary; although, as she mentioned later, some people needed a little more persuasion to volunteer than others. Thando had needed no persuasion at all: he jumped out of the kombi when it pulled up on the pavement outside the house, brandishing his old placard that read, "I have the right to say no to violence."

"I speak for the trees!" he announced to the street and made a power salute.

"Thando," said Mrs. Pruitt. "Remember what I told you all: no violence."

"No violence?" said JJ. "But I'm only here for the violence."

"No, you are not, JJ. Discipline, dignity, and restraint are what we want. Discipline, dignity, and restraint. Discipline, dignity, and restraint." She chanted it as if it might catch on like a punchy rallying cry but no one took it up.

"That doesn't sound very interesting," said Yolanda,

speaking sideways out of her mouth.

"It'll be plenty interesting," said Mrs. Pruitt. "I promise you. With you lot, that's virtually guaranteed."

Mercy left Mrs. Pruitt to get everyone assembled while she wheeled her bike to the carport. She was relieved to see that Mr. Craven had not yet arrived. But Mrs. Mullins was there sitting in a canvas deck chair under the camel's foot tree. She had a cardboard box beside her. On the box was a cup of tea and three rock cakes on a plate.

"You've brought backup," Mrs. Mullins said, waving at Mrs. Pruitt. "Excellent. I'm in charge of the camel foot tree. I'll wrap my arms around it and refuse to let go. And good luck to them if they manage to lift me." She laughed heartily and her many chins wobbled. "It will be like trying to lift a stove!"

"He might even have to use the Bobcat!" Mr. Singh's voice emerged from the other side of the path with a chuckle, but Mercy could not see him until Mrs. Mullins pointed up at his thin legs dangling from the lower branches of the pecan nut tree.

"I've brought some friends from school to help," Mercy called up into the tree.

"I can see!" said Mr. Singh. "And it makes my heart sing to see so many lovely young people come to our aid. Let me come down and greet them. Just pick up the step ladder for me, Mercy, and put it against the tree."

The step ladder had been kicked away from the tree and lay sprawled on its side.

"Oooh, it's not very com-fitable up there." Mr. Singh rubbed his bottom when he was down on the ground. "I should have taken a cushion." He hobbled over on his bandy legs to shake Mrs. Pruitt's hand.

Just as Mercy was introducing Mrs. Pruitt and Mr. Singh, there was a reek of diesel and a roar of engine: Mr. Craven had arrived. In the back of the truck were two workers wearing blue overalls. They both had visors, chainsaws, and big leather gloves.

Mr. Craven, wearing a black overall, stood on the pavement, hands on his hips, staring at the extraordinary number of people in the garden. He counted heads and he looked at his truck cabin. There was no way fourteen people were going to fit inside that.

"Is this your doing, Missy?" he asked Mercy. "Huh, Missy? All these people? You think this is going to stop me?" He took out his cell. "I can just phone my friend who runs a private security firm to come and take…"

"Good morning," said Mr. Singh. "I'm assuming you have brought the official paper work that confirms that you have the right to start the demolition of the garden?"

Mr. Craven rolled his eyes and turned to rummage in the cubbyhole of his truck. He produced a sheaf of papers and waved them above his head. "Ja, I've got papers," he said. "If you want to be stupid about it."

"Let me have a look at those," said Mr. Singh, stretching out his hand.

"You don't trust me?" Mr. Craven started putting the papers back in the cubbyhole.

"I'd just like to see those papers, please," said Mr. Singh politely. He took a step closer to Mr. Craven. So did Mrs. Pruitt.

Mr. Craven threw the papers at them and strode off to start instructing his workers.

Mercy picked up the papers that had fluttered to the ground. She handed them to Mr. Singh and Mrs. Pruitt and went to join her classmates in the garden.

Thando, JJ, and Yolanda had swung themselves up into the branches of the pecan nut tree. Olive and Jameela had linked arms and were standing defiant in front of the-pride- of-India. Everyone else was sitting on the front steps, waiting for instruction or to see what would happen next.

"So is this your house, Mercy?" asked Beatrice. She puffed sideways out of her mouth to blow her fringe out of her eyes.

"Yes. Why?"

"No, nothing." She smiled and shrugged. "It's...cute. Sort of old fashioned." She wrinkled her nose. "I love it. But it might be better to just knock it down and build something more, like, modern?"

Mercy noticed Nelisiwe's eyes widen just a little bit at the comment and glance at Mercy as if to say, "Sorry about that."

"*Oweh!*" Nelisiwe jumped off the step and wrapped her arms around the trunk of the old wisteria that framed the sitting room bay window. One of the workers was approaching it with a chainsaw. He stopped in his tracks, uncertain.

"*Iyeke mnganewami,*" said Nelisiwe to the worker.

"You speak Xhosa?" asked the worker.

"*Ewe,*" said Nelisiwe. "Please, uncle, leave the tree."

"OK *ungusis wam'*." He turned away to find another tree to cut, but each one was marked and guarded.

Mercy felt a glow that started in her middle and spread out. She was not alone.

Then there was a shout from near the camel's foot tree. Mrs. Mullins had aimed a rock cake at Dumisani as he tried to get the Bobcat started. He rubbed his head and started to laugh.

"It's not bladdy funny," shouted Mr. Craven, tossing the truck keys at Dumisani. "Stop laughing and get the jump leads out of the truck."

"Excuse me. These so-called papers," said Mr. Singh. "This one is an electricity account and these three," he held up the papers in his fist, "are old traffic fines."

Mr. Craven turned and walked away. He stood with his back to the garden, looking at the road, and pulled out his cell phone again. Everyone, including the workers, stopped what they were doing and watched him. He dialed a number and kicked a pebble on the pavement so it pinged off the hubcap of his truck.

"Hey, Lloyd. Howzit man? Ja, it's me. We got a situation here. Ja, in Hodson Road. So can you get some okes to come and help me here? Ja, exactly. Only worse. Like fourteen? Bring the...you know. Ja, definitely. OK, cheers."

Mr. Craven put the phone back in his pocket and looked at his watch. He crossed his arms and sat on the low wall to wait with his back to everyone. Dumisani and the other worker got spanners out of the truck and went back to work, tinkering with the metal plate over the backside of the Bobcat to get at the battery.

Mr. Singh consulted with Mrs. Pruitt and Mrs. Mullins. Mrs. Pruitt took out her cell phone and also made a call. Then they summoned everyone together under the pecan nut tree. Yolanda, Thando, and JJ swung out of the branches to join them.

Mr. Singh told them that they didn't know what to expect, but under no circumstances was anyone to fight back.

"What must we do if one of those guys tries to pick me up? Can't I kick him?" asked JJ.

"No. Just stand there. Don't do anything," said Mr. Singh.

"It's easy," said Thando. "Don't just do something! Stand there!"

Everyone looked at Thando. "Exactly," said Mrs. Mullins eventually. "Sharp boy that."

"If anyone tries to pick you up, just go floppy and do not resist," said Mrs. Pruitt. "The police are on their way. Remember Mr. Craven is breaking the law by demolishing this garden—and we have done nothing wrong in trying to stop him."

Several people practiced being floppy by leaning against one another. "Oops, sorry, Missy," said Thando as he leaned against Mercy, who staggered and fell against Olive, who fell against Jameela. When everyone lay in a laughing tangled heap on the ground, JJ did a running jump and flung himself so he was spread-eagled over everyone.

"That's enough," said Mrs. Pruitt pulling him off the pile. "Remember what I said, JJ? No violence."

"Aaah, that's no fun," said JJ and he punched Thando as he got up laughing from the ground.

"I understand the temptation, JJ," said Mrs. Pruitt as she held his arm firmly at his side and looked into his eyes. "Believe me, I do."

CHAPTER 44

"Let us sing," said Mrs. Mullins. "Something rousing to stir the spirits while we await our fate." And she lifted up her many chins and broke into song:

Land of hope and glory, mother of the free
How shall we extol thee, who are born of thee?

Mrs. Pruitt hummed along with her. *"Dum dum dum-dum dum DUUUM dum..."*

But the effect was not rousing.

"Doesn't someone know a good protest song?" asked Mrs. Pruitt.

Nelisiwe and Beatrice began to shake their hands and gyrate.

Baby, I'm just gonna shake, shake, shake, shake, shake
I shake it off, I shake it off...

"Oh no," said Mrs. Pruitt. "Not this nonsense again." She put out her hand to steady JJ who had joined in the shaking so much that it looked as if he was having an epileptic fit. "Something South African please." With her other hand, she removed Thando's placard from off of him as he was shaking it around under the tree and causing a cascade of leaves like green glitter at a talent contest.

Then, as if from nowhere, Nelisiwe's voice rose clean and pure as an arrow shot straight through the tree and up into the blue sky:

SENZENINA, Senzenina, Senzenina...

Then two deep baritone voices joined in from under the camel's foot tree. Mr. Craven's workers were doing a slow dance with one fist raised. "SENZENINA," they harmonized. The effect was rich, slow, and powerful. Everyone stood transfixed; even Mr. Craven stood up to watch.

"Senzenina," Nelisiwe sang.

"Senzenina," they responded. "Senzenina."

"Senzenina kulomhlaba?"

"What does it mean?" whispered Mrs. Mullins to Mr. Singh who was swaying to the sound of the old protest song with his eyes closed.

"It means 'What have we done? What have we done? What have we done to this earth?'" he replied. "Oh, I love this song. It takes me back to those old days of fighting apartheid."

Mrs. Mullins put up her hand for Mr. Singh to help her out of the deck chair, and, once standing, she swayed from side to side in time to the music. Mercy noticed Mrs. Pruitt link arms with Mr. Singh and join in. It was impossible not to be swept away by the great rolling swell of the tune as it billowed out across the garden, rising and falling on a great tide of emotion.

Senzenina, Senzenina

Mercy closed her eyes and just listened to the singing.

But the moment was rudely interrupted.

"What's this?" shouted Mr. Craven. "You think you at blimming church or something? You stop this *kak* right now and get that battery working—or you both fired."

He pointed at his workers with a chainsaw, then swung it over his shoulder like a huge machine gun, stepped over the fence into the vacant plot, and headed straight for the wild pear tree.

Mercy, Thando, and Olive started after him but Mr. Singh held them back.

"No, stay here." Then he shouted over the fence: "Mr. Craven, be careful! There's a bee..."

But the rest of his words were cut into tiny flying shards by the roar of the chainsaw.

"What's going on?" shouted Thando over the racket.

But before Mercy could answer, the chainsaw cut out. There were a few moments of silence then...

"Bees!" screamed Mr. Craven. "Bees! I'm getting... STUNG!"

"Oh my godfathers," said Mrs. Mullins.

Mr. Craven ran for the safety of the truck. He was swatting at bees as he ran, his arms flailing around like an inflatable tube man in a high wind. Mercy could see the bees from where she stood. They formed a crust on his back and others were following him like a small brown cloud. He got to the truck and yanked at the doors but they were locked. Desperately, he dug in his pockets. His face was already starting to swell from the bites.

"Help!"

"*Nakhu!*" Dumisani shouted, digging for the keys in the pockets of his overalls. Mr. Singh grabbed them and ran to the truck. The doors unlocked but Mr. Craven was writhing on the road with his arms covering his face. Mr. Singh flinched as bees flew in his face. Somehow he dragged Mr. Craven up off the tarmac and into the cab. Then he got up into the cab himself and slammed the door shut.

"Oh Mr. Singh," said Mercy and she covered her mouth with one hand as if she could keep the horror from escaping. Mrs. Pruitt put her arm around her and pulled her close.

Behind her, she could hear Beatrice saying in breathless little puffs: "Oh my God! He is so going to get stung! Oh my God!"

She could see Mr. Singh swiping at bees from inside the truck cab. Every now and then, he wound down the window, flicked bees off his hand, and wound the window back up quickly.

Mr. Craven was sitting still and upright in the seat. His face was swollen beyond all recognition.

"Grade 6 get inside the house. Now." Mrs. Pruitt spoke with force and everyone did as they were told without arguing.

CHAPTER 45

"That's fifteen stings I've counted so far," said Aunt Mary. She was scraping the stings carefully off Mr. Singh with a kitchen knife while he sat at the kitchen table.

"Iff not the beesh' fault," said Mr. Singh, speaking thickly through swollen lips.

"I think it was because Mr. Craven threatened them with the noise of the chainsaw," said Mercy. "Plus he was wearing dark colors so maybe the bees thought he was a honey badger."

Aunt Mary and Mr. de Wet, accompanied by a lawyer, had arrived home to chaos, or, in Aunt Mary's words, "absolute pandemonium." Paramedics were helping Mr. Craven into the back of an ambulance; the garden was full of schoolchildren; and four men dressed in black from their helmets to their boots were arguing with a policeman and Mrs. Mullins on the pavement.

There was a long line of cars all the way down Hodson Road: an ambulance, a police car, a private security van, a school bus, and a truck.

"Mercy, just go and check if the private security storm troopers have left yet?" said Aunt Mary. She dotted Mr.

Singh's stings with a paste made of baking powder and water. "I cannot stand to have them on the property."

Mercy went out onto the veranda to check. Mrs. Mullins stood on the pavement with her hands on her hips, the lawyer beside her. There was no sign of the private security men or their van emblazoned with the words *Viper Enforce Security*.

But there was a new car in its place and a woman with lots of curly hair and a notebook was talking to Mrs. Pruitt.

"Hey, Missy!" called Thando from under the pecan nut tree. "Come." He summoned her with a hoop of his hand. "This guy wants to take our photo for the paper."

Missy? Well, at least Thando hadn't heard Mr. Craven calling her "Misery" or "Messy." Mercy went to join them.

"Come and stand next to me," said Beatrice. "Fame at last." She fluffed out her hair and put her face right up against Mercy's. Before Mercy could pull away, she felt Beatrice's cheek bulge in a big wide smile—and then the photographer clicked.

It turned out that it was Mr. de Wet who had called the newspaper, hoping to strengthen their case with a bit of publicity. It took a while for the journalist to get the full story and by the time she had interviewed the aunts, Mr. Singh, Mrs. Mullins, Mrs. Pruitt, the children, the lawyer, and Mr. Craven's workers, it was past lunch time and everyone was hungry. So Mrs. Pruitt made a big pot of tea and the children gathered in the sitting room to share out Mrs. Mullins' enormous tin of rock cakes. Aunt Mary had just taken a sip of tea and leaned back in her chair when..."Hello, hello?" another voice called from the veranda and tapped politely with the knocker.

"Oh for crying in a bucket! And who could this be?" Aunt Mary put her tea cup down and got up to investigate.

Mercy had a mouth full of rock cake. She stopped chewing to listen. She recognized the voice and it turned the rock cake to ash in her mouth. It was Mrs. Naidoo!

Aunt Mary put her head round the door of the sitting room. "Mrs. Pruitt, do you have a minute? There's a social worker here who would like a word with you. Perhaps we can all meet in the kitchen."

Mercy closed her eyes. She sat with her back to the wall, immobilized with dread.

A few minutes later she felt a warm hand on her shoulder. Aunt Mary was smiling down at her.

"It's all fine, Mercy." Aunt Mary lay her hand on Mercy's head. "Mrs. Naidoo went to school today, saw your excellent school reports, and had a word with Mrs. Griesel. Now Mrs. Pruitt is busy telling her that you are a model student and that you are much loved by everyone."

"She's not going to move me to a place of safety?" Mercy whispered.

"Not at all. What could be safer than this house? Defended by friends, neighbors, and all those who love you. Though perhaps it's a good thing she didn't arrive half an hour ago when the air was thick with bees."

"Greetings," boomed another voice from the veranda.

"Come in," called Aunt Mary. "We are receiving visits from all and sundry today! We are in the sitting room."

Doctor Waku stooped as he entered the door. He held a small hat in his spade-like hand.

"Greetings, greetings." He nodded at everyone in the room. "I see you have lots of helpers."

"Yes, weren't we lucky?" And Aunt Mary filled him in

on all the developments: the interdict, the lawyer who arrived to verify the details, the police who accompanied Mr. Craven to be kept under police custody in the hospital, and the private security company that had been sent packing by Mrs. Mullins.

"And now we even have a social worker chatting to Mercy's teacher in the kitchen."

"This is excellent news," he said. "But tell me, where were the birds?"

"The birds?" asked Aunt Mary. "You mean the bees? The bees were very helpful today in this little drama."

"No, no, the birds. I know this, because the ancestors are telling me that you will be rescued by the birds."

"Not the bees? Are you sure?"

"It is the birds. Of that I am certain."

"How very odd," said Aunt Mary.

Mercy and Aunt Mary stood on the pavement as everyone climbed back in the school bus. She held tightly onto Aunt Mary's hand: there was such a lightness in her heart, she felt she might float straight into the sky like a helium balloon. She noticed that Olive sat in the front seat near the driver and she saw Jameela climb in and sit beside her. They looked down and laughed together about something she couldn't see. Then Olive looked up at Mercy with a radiant smiling face and waved.

Nelisiwe climbed on the bus and sat next to Beatrice. Beatrice said something, rolled her eyes, and laughed. Then, Mercy noticed with some surprise, Nelisiwe got up and moved to the seat in front of her, next to Thando who was leaning out the window: "Miss McKnight, any time you want someone to come and not cut down trees in your garden, I'm your guy," he said.

"I'll remember that, young man. Thank you."

"Hey, Missy. See you tomorrow." He grinned at Mercy.

She felt her insides go flip-flop and the color rise in her cheeks. So she bent down quickly to scratch her foot, hoping that by the time she stood up straight, the feeling would pass.

But it didn't.

CHAPTER 46

In the days that followed the "absolute pandemonium," Mercy returned home from school each afternoon to find the house crawling with people. Usually she could hear the tick of the clock, the hum of the fridge, and the lazy buzz of flies at the window. But this week there were the sounds of boots tramping in the roof; of banging, hammering, dropping, and dragging; and of voices in every room.

Mr. Singh's brother-in-law and his two nephews were on the roof; an electrician was fiddling with the electrical mains board in the scullery; on two occasions, there was a lawyer in the sitting room and a policeman at the kitchen table taking a statement. Doctor Waku loaded all the chopped branches and took them away in his van and Mr. de Wet strode in and out of the house talking loudly about Telkom, electrical circuits, ceiling boards, and cheap Harvey tiles.

Aunt Mary seemed confident that all these repairs would be paid for by Mr. Craven after she'd taken him to court. The lawyer seemed to think she could sue him for damages.

"But we'll still have to really tighten our belts," said Aunt

Mary. "There won't be any money for jam once I've paid for Flora's care."

On Friday afternoon, Mercy helped Mr. Singh drag the boxes that had been taken out of the roof so that they formed an orderly line down the passage. Someone was coming on Monday to replace the damaged ceiling boards. Mercy lifted up the flaps of one box to find three old black photo albums with tiny black and white photos between pages of tissue paper, a green casserole dish with a glass lid, and some lumpy things wrapped in a moth-eaten wool cardigan.

Then she heard Mrs. Pruitt's voice calling from the front door.

"Helloooo. Hellooo. Anyone home?"

"Angela!" called Aunt Mary from the sitting room. "Come in. You'll have to excuse the mess."

Angela? Mercy had never imagined that Mrs. Pruitt had a first name. Though she had noticed that Aunt Mary had stopped calling her "poor Mrs. Pruitt" and referred to her now as "that marvelous Mrs. Pruitt."

"I've just popped in to see how you are all doing," Mercy heard Mrs. Pruitt say. "And to show you this from the Maritzburg Mirror in case you haven't seen it."

"Mercy," called Aunt Mary. "Come and see. You're in the newspaper."

Mercy went through to the kitchen, wiping her dusty hands on her leggings. She took the newspaper carefully.

The photo was a surprise. The most noticeable face, and the person who looked the happiest, was Beatrice—which proved that photos could be so deceiving. Mercy's own face looked unremarkable. The caption gave all their names and quoted Mrs. Pruitt as saying that their "involvement was part of a school project on responsible citizenship and a practical example of passive resistance."

"A school project. Responsible citizenship," said Aunt Mary. "Aren't words splendid? They can make anything, even that chaos, sound thoroughly educational."

Mrs. Pruitt laughed.

"Mercy, why don't you show Mrs. Pruitt the garden while I get the kettle boiling? She might like to see Lemon's grave."

Mrs. Pruitt knelt down under the fig tree to see the small mound of earth. Mercy had put fresh flowers there that morning and marked the edge with little round stones. The two birds continued to stand guard over the mealie pips in the cup of a withering leaf.

"What are these?" asked Mrs. Pruitt. She touched the birds' heads.

"Lids. Aunt Mary says her dad used to keep his tobacco in jars and these went on top."

"May I have a look?"

"Yes."

Mrs. Pruitt sat back on her haunches with a bird's head cradled in each hand. She examined them closely from every angle.

"You don't have the tobacco jars?"

"No, I think they are lost."

"Would you mind if I take them inside? We can put them back later. I just want to chat to Aunt Mary about them."

And so in the end, it was the birds that ended up rescuing them, just as Doctor Waku had foretold.

"These heads are from tobacco jars called Wally Birds

made by Victorian potters called the Martin Brothers. They were made in about 1880 or 1890 and are very collectible items," said Mrs. Pruitt as she put them carefully on a folded tea towel on the kitchen table. "If you can find the bodies that form the jars, they could be worth a lot of money."

"How extraordinary," said Aunt Mary. "My mother gave them to my father as a gift. Her sister Winifred, who was a bit of a bohemian—she liked to wear a turban—left the jars to my mother in her will. My mother always thought they were ugly, but my father rather..."

"How much money?" asked Mercy.

"I know that one sold at Sotheby's in London a few years ago for forty thousand pounds," said Mrs. Pruitt. "So two big Wally Birds, like these, could be worth about...oh, I don't know, it's hard to guess. Maybe one and half million rand? Maybe less, maybe more."

"I know where to look." Mercy slipped into the passage. As she knelt by the box, her hands trembled as she lifted out the lumpy objects wrapped in the dusty cardigan, scattering dust and tiny granular fish moth eggs.

Each jar had a circular wooden base, gripped by great talons that supported golden-brown feathered bodies, finely worked and textured. When Mercy held them to her nose, she inhaled the deep rich smell of tobacco.

It was the smell of something old and protective, of safety. It was the smell of home.

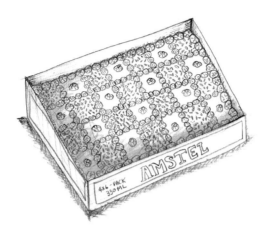

CHAPTER 47

On the last day of term, Mrs. Pruitt baked a chocolate cake and brought it to class in a beer box lined with tin foil. She had to put it up on the book cupboard, out of reach, to stop people from walking past and pinching the chunks of Cadbury Flake that she'd scattered over the icing. A few people still had to do their orals on role models and then there was going to be a farewell party for Mrs. Pruitt in the classroom. The paper cups were all lined up on Mrs. Pruitt's desk ready for the cooldrink to be poured.

Mercy sat at her desk with a small stack of notes in front of her. She tried to read them through once more, but the conversations around her kept intruding.

"OK, so ask your mom to bring you at lunch time on Saturday." Olive was talking to Jameela about visiting over the weekend. Mercy had been invited but was going to visit Aunt Flora so couldn't go.

"Nelisiwe, do you want to come too? We're going to make pizzas in our new pizza oven."

"Ja, sure," said Nelisiwe. "Will you have bacon and pine-apple? That's my favorite."

"Bacon and pineapple?" said Beatrice. "Eeeuw! That's so

gross. It's probably the worst kind of pizza *ever.*"

Mercy was aware that Beatrice had not been invited to the pizza party. She felt a tiny bit sorry for her, but her overwhelming instinct was still to avoid Beatrice as much as possible. Since the day when everyone came to protect the trees in the garden, Beatrice had become friends with some girls in Grade 7. She looked as if she could barely tolerate her own classmates and never missed an opportunity to tell them how immature they were. Most of her venom was now directed at Nelisiwe who had made new friends. Aunt Mary had once told Mercy that ridicule often looked and felt like a weapon, but usually it was a shield. She said people who make fun of others a lot are trying to protect themselves. At the time Mercy had not really understood, but now she was starting to get a sense that Beatrice's nasty comments were most likely a way of trying to appear strong when inside she was probably feeling scared. Was everyone scared? Mercy wondered. Even Beatrice Hunter?

"Time for the last few orals." Mrs. Pruitt clapped her hands and brought everyone to attention. Mercy's heart lurched.

"JJ, you're up."

JJ gave his oral on Candice Swanepoel, the supermodel. He said that he admired her because, although she was born in Mooi River, South Africa, she regularly appears on lists for the hundred sexiest women in the world. Plus she was once chosen to model the "fantasy bra" for the Victoria Secret Fashion Show. He slapped a picture he'd cut of a magazine on the board. It showed a blond woman in a pair of red pants and a bra encrusted with jewels.

"And is this something you want to do one day?" asked

Mrs. Pruitt when he'd finished.

JJ looked confused. "Obviously not."

"OK, thanks, JJ. You can return to your seat." Mrs. Pruitt looked down at her list of names.

Mercy could hardly breathe. Her name was last on the list.

"Where's my excuse note, Mercy?" asked Mrs. Pruitt, smiling as she peered over spectacles with her hand held out.

"I don't have one, Mrs. Pruitt." Mercy walked the long mile to the front of the classroom and put her notes on the table so that her shaking hands wouldn't be so visible.

"Good morning," she said in a tight, tiny voice. "As you can see, I am very nervous to do this. So I have written out my oral..." She swallowed and licked her dry lips"...which I will try to read."

Mr. Singh said that there was nothing wrong with telling people that you are nervous. "Tell the truth," he said to her. "Even if your voice shakes."

Mercy looked at Mrs. Pruitt who nodded and smiled. Then she glanced quickly at Thando. He was leaning forward in his chair, hands gripped together, willing her on.

Thando had told her a trick: "If you are nervous about public speaking, picture your audience with no clothes on. Or if that doesn't work, imagine everyone on the toilet."

But when she looked up, everyone was sitting fully clothed on chairs. To undress them and place each person mentally on a toilet seat took more concentration than she had to spare. Every bit of effort was going into reading the pages in front of her. And this was what she read:

"As you know, I was going to do my role model oral on Mahatma Gandhi who began his life of activism right here

in Pietermaritzburg. Once when Gandhi stepped off a train in India, his sandal fell between the train and the platform and he couldn't get it back. So he took off his other sandal and threw it down too. When people asked him why he did that, he explained that one sandal was no use to anyone. It was better that someone finds two sandals on the track than just one. This taught me to look at problems with new eyes."

Mercy stopped and took a deep breath. Mr. Singh had told her to read slowly, but she was worried that the slower she read, the more everyone would hear the shake in her voice.

"This week we have heard many stories about famous people. And even a chicken."

"Mike, my chicken!" said Thando as he gave a power salute. Everyone laughed.

"Settle down everyone," said Mrs. Pruitt. "Sorry, Mercy, please continue."

So she did...

"But I have decided that I'm not going to do my oral on a person—although I do admire Gandhi very much. I will be doing my oral today on African Honey Bees. There are many interesting facts about bees but I am only going to tell you about the lessons they have taught me."

Mr. Singh had told her that it was important to look up and make eye contact with her audience when she spoke. So Mercy risked a peep at the class. Mrs. Pruitt was writing something in her book. Everyone else looked interested, as if they were really listening to her. Everyone that was except Beatrice, who was whispering, "Bees? Did she say *bees*?" to anyone who would listen, as if she couldn't believe what she was hearing.

Mercy took another deep breath and continued...

"Every bee has a job to do—some collect nectar, some protect the hive, some feed the baby bees, and some flap their wings to keep the right temperature in the hive. No one job is more important than another. In our human hive, most of us will never be the queen bee. There can only be one Nelson Mandela or Mahatma Gandhi. But without the work done by all the ordinary people, our human hive, like the beehive, will not survive."

Out of the corner of her eye, Mercy could see Mrs. Pruitt nodding as she jotted down notes. Mercy plowed on, hoping that no one would see her legs shaking from behind the desk. She dreaded having to flip the pages of her notes, because of the tremor in her hands.

"The other thing I have learned is that bees work very hard. Working together, a whole hive of bees will fly about three times round the world to produce about one kilogram of honey. And a single bee will only produce one twelfth of a teaspoon of honey in its whole life. It's the same with the work done by people. There are lots of different jobs that people do—and they are all important especially when they help to make the world a little bit easier and a little bit sweeter for others. But doing those jobs will always be hard work."

Mrs. Pruitt had put down her pen and was just listening, smiling, and nodding. It made Mercy feel braver but her voice was still shaky and often she had to swallow in inconvenient places. Her mouth felt dry.

"I have also learned that bees, as they go about collecting nectar to feed their hive, are also, without knowing it, rubbing pollen from one flower onto another. If bees didn't do this work, no fruit, flowers, or vegetables would get pollinated.

It is the same with the small things we do—one small act can make other, much bigger things happen. We don't always know what that is going to be. But we must do those things anyway."

Mercy just had one more point to make and then she was finished.

"The last thing I have learned about bees is that it really takes guts for them to protect their hive. I say this because when a bee stings you, it leaves behind some of its guts with the sting. Bits of its abdomen get pulled out of its body and that actually kills the bee."

"Cool!" interrupted JJ, who was looking especially interested in this part of Mercy's oral. "So that's why the bee dies?"

Mercy nodded.

"Carry on, Mercy," said Mrs. Pruitt, "now that you've got JJ's attention with a bit of death and destruction."

Mercy took one last deep breath and finished:

"In the same way, when we do something brave, it takes our guts, something deep inside that feels almost like it is a part of us. Luckily for us we don't die when we do it, though it might feel as if we will.

I hope you have enjoyed my talk about bees and what they have taught me. Thank you."

There was silence. Mrs. Pruitt blew her nose. Then Thando puffed air out of his cheeks as if he'd been holding his breath.

Mrs. Pruitt said, "I think that was maybe the best oral I have ever heard." She smiled broadly at Mercy. "Now let's eat that cake."

CHAPTER 48

Six months later, Mercy was in the kitchen bottling honey to sell at the Grade 6 Market Day. She was cranking the handle of an old honey extractor that had been found in a box in the roof when the new ceiling boards had been put in.

Discovering the contents of those boxes had been like finding buried treasure. The Wally birds had fetched a lot of money at an auction in Cape Town, although Aunt Mary would not tell Mercy how much.

"Enough money for a lot of jam," was all she would say.

Inside the other boxes, they had also discovered a rusty cheese grater and some casserole dishes, as well as all the bits of the old fountain that Aunt Flora believed had been stolen. The fountain, including the tubular bit that Aunt Flora had once tried to give to King George, had been reassembled in the garden to the left of the footpath. Mr. Singh had got the water piped across to the fountain and the sound of it trickling on a hot day was, in Aunt Mary's words, "just heavenly." It was a memorial to Aunt Flora, who was still alive but spending her remaining days in a tall bed in a bright sunny room of the Frail Care section of the Old Age

Home. They visited her often to stroke her hands and comb her fluffy hair, but she did not appear to recognize anyone.

Mercy was telling Mr. Singh that her nice new teacher Mr. Ngidi had already ordered two jars of honey for himself when there was a knock on the front door. She still had the old fear that a social worker would arrive to say that family members had been found and wanted to take her away—so she stopped cranking to hold her breath and listen. She heard Aunt Mary greet the person in a low careful voice.

It took Mercy a few seconds to recognize the person who walked into the kitchen that day.

"Mercy?" The woman smiled as if trying to hold back the joy that would come bursting out of her if she opened her lips even a crack. Her eyes were brimming with tears.

"It's your Aunty Kathleen," said Aunt Mary gently when Mercy didn't move.

"I know," said Mercy and she flew into her aunt's open arms. "Where have you been? Oh, where have you been?"

"I've been away in a very dark place," said Aunty Kathleen with her face buried in Mercy's hair. "But I've left Uncle Clifford and I have found myself a good job. It's been a very hard time. I need to tell you...one day I'll tell you about your Uncle Clifford and about why I've stayed away from you all these years. But for now all you need to know is I love you; you are my sister's precious child and I've found you..." Aunty Kathleen pushed Mercy away to look at her face. "Look at you! I saw your picture in the newspaper. So grown up and looking so much like my dear Rose it breaks my heart. There's so much to tell, I don't know where to start."

"Let me put the kettle on and make us some tea," said Aunt Mary.

And Mercy saw that, although she had no idea where it

would lead, she, once again, just had to do the job that was right in front of her.

She took Aunty Kathleen's hand. "Come and sit here," Mercy said, pulling out the chair where Aunt Flora had always sat at the kitchen table. "Do you want honey in your tea?"

"Oh yes," said Aunty Kathleen. "I love honey. Thank you."

"I harvested this myself," said Mercy as she put the jar of honey on the table.

"Yes," said Aunty Kathleen and she smiled at Mercy with so much love and pride. "Yes. I can imagine you did."

THE END

Gandhi: his early life and his time in South Africa

Mohandas Karamchand Gandhi was born in Porbandar in India in 1869 to Hindu parents. His mother was very devout and strong minded and Gandhi always spoke of her as a powerful influence in his life. But his childhood showed little indication of the extraordinary man that he became. He was a fearful child—terrified of darkness, serpents, and ghosts and at school he was, by his own admission, "an average student." He was very shy and he didn't enjoy sport.

When he finished school his family scraped together money to send him to England to study law, but when he returned home to India three years later, he found it difficult to make a good living: he lacked the confidence that was needed to stand up in court, question witnesses, and present an argument. So, when he was offered the chance to go to South Africa and represent an Indian businessman in a legal dispute, he took it, hoping that he would earn some money and gain experience and confidence.

Gandhi arrived in South Africa in 1893 and was shocked by what he found. Indian people had come to South Africa in the 1860's to work as indentured laborers on sugar plantations, on the railways, and in the mines. The deal was that workers would work for five years and then be allowed to get a small piece of land and settle. But by 1891 the offer of land and citizenship was revoked, so most Indian people lived without land or rights and suffered many hardships and indignities. They lived in terrible conditions, were badly paid, and not given enough to eat. In the Transvaal,

Indian workers were not allowed to own land except for small plots in ghettos; they did not have the vote; could not walk on the pavement; and were not allowed out at night without permission.

Gandhi's experience in South Africa did prove to be profoundly transforming in ways that he could not have imagined: on a cold night in June 1893 he was thrown off a train in Pietermaritzburg on his way to Pretoria to defend his client. He was traveling in a first-class compartment and a white passenger complained that he didn't want to share his compartment with "a second class citizen." Later in his life when someone asked him what was the most important experience of his life, he said that it was the night that he was forced to spend in the Pietermaritzburg waiting room. Because that was the night that "the iron entered his soul." He decided to stay in South Africa, resist this outrageous discrimination, finish his work, and not go back to India, which was his instinct. So in the morning he bought another first-class train ticket and proceeded to Pretoria. It was the first of many times that he took the decision to resist injustice rather than turn away.

In the end Gandhi spent 21 years in South Africa.

- ๕ He unified Indian people by helping to form the Natal Indian Congress in 1894 which drew attention to the many hardships that Indian people suffered.

- ๕ He started a newspaper called *Indian Opinion* that also helped to draw attention to the problems of indentured Indians all over the world.

- ๕ In 1906 he developed his method of resistance called *Satyagraha*. In Sanscrit *Satya* means "truth"; *agraha* means "holding firmly to" or "polite insistence." Gandhi used this method of resistance to protest against many unjust laws. He encouraged people to refuse to co-operate with laws that did not serve the truth that all people are created equal. The resistance was to be non-violent. His followers were warned that their actions might result in the confiscation of property, imprisonment, flogging, starvation or even death. He urged them to accept these consequences without complaint because Gandhi believed that there was no other way to achieve justice. *"The struggle might last a long time. But I can boldly declare, and with certainty, that so long as there is even a handful of men true to their pledge, there can only be one end to the struggle—and that is victory."*

ℬ Gandhi was arrested 4 times while he was in South Africa. He spent many months in solitary confinement and was often made to do hard labor.

ℬ During one of his imprisonments, Gandhi made General Smuts (who had authorized his arrest) a pair of leather sandals. Smuts returned the sandals to Gandhi on Gandhi's seventieth birthday and remarked, *"I have worn these sandals for many a summer...even though I may feel that I am not worthy to stand in the shoes of so great a man. It was my fate to be the antagonist of a man for whom even then I had the highest respect.... He never forgot the human background of the situation, never lost his temper or succumbed to hate, and preserved his gentle humor even in the most trying situations."*

In 1914 Gandhi returned home to India with his family. He applied what he'd learned in South Africa to a much bigger task: the freedom of India, which was at that time a colony in the enormous and powerful British Empire. The method of *satyagraha* eventually brought the British Empire to its knees and India got her independence in 1947. Gandhi was assassinated in 1949 but his powerful message of nonviolent resistance lives on and has influenced every civil rights movement since then.

Interesting facts about bees

There are lots of books and websites that describe bees: their lifecycle, colonies, and anatomy. The list below contains just some of the lesser known facts about these fascinating insects:

- There are 20, 000 different kinds of bees in the world and most of them are solitary: they live by themselves and raise their young alone. Honeybees, however, live in colonies that may contain as many as 60 thousand bees.

- Honeybees can be divided into 3 groups:
  - Workers are all female. Each bee will take on different duties depending on her age. Young worker bees do the house work: cleaning, nursing the larvae, keeping the hive at the right temperature, carrying food and making wax. Slightly older bees guard the nest and sting any bees, wasps, or other insects that are not part of their colony. The oldest bees become foragers and collect nectar and pollen.
  - Drones are all male. They have only one function: to mate once with the Queen bee, after which they die. They cannot feed themselves because their tongues are too short to reach the nectar inside flowers.
  - The Queen Bee is the biggest bee because she is fed on a rich substance called royal jelly. She mates

once in her life and is fertilized by about 20 drones. She stores the sperm in her body and uses it to lay 1500 eggs a day.

- Foragers travel distances of up to 2 miles to collect nectar and pollen. If a bee finds a good source of food, she returns to the colony and does a little dance to communicate with other bees where to go. A round dance is done to show that food is close by. A waggle dance communicates the distance and the direction of a more distant food source.

- A bee's brain is the size of a sesame seed, yet it is capable of complex calculations involving distance and foraging efficiency. Bees navigate using the sun and never get lost.

- They need pollen to get protein. They carry the pollen back to the hive in little pollen baskets on their legs. They also sip nectar from flowers which is stored in the bee's honey stomach.

- When a forager bee gets home to the colony, she transfers the nectar into the mouth of a house bee where it mixes with enzymes (bee spit). Eventually when there is the right mix of nectar and enzymes, it gets deposited in a wax cell. House bees then fan the cell to evaporate the water. Only when it's the correct consistency for honey does it get capped with a layer of wax.

- A single bee working all its life will collect enough nectar to make a twelfth of a teaspoon of honey.

- Honey does not easily decompose. Honey found in an Egyptian tomb was still edible after 3000 years.

- Flowers need bees for pollination as much as bees need flowers. Flowers use fragrance, color, and an electrical charge to draw bees to them.

Thanks

You'd think writing a book is a solitary activity, but it looks like it took a village to write this one.

Thank you to my writing group for years of tea and cake in the Bots and for plodding through really bad first drafts of this story, but always remaining optimistic and kind: Moraig Peden, Fiona Jackson, and Marie Odendaal. Heartfelt thanks too to Kath Magrobi and to Liz Mattson for helping me to polish this into something readable. Your friendship, faith, and good ideas helped in ways too many to mention. Thank you, Hilary Kromberg, for being my secret agent and for setting this little miracle in motion. Thank you, Marie and Fiona Matheson, for letting me use your lovely house as the setting for this story. Thank you, Sharon and Kelly, for sharing your experiences on fostering children and to Ramona Alexander from The Unicorn's Haven for your insights into Alzheimer's.

And thank you to all these kind people who shared their expertise: the late Juliet Armstrong for Martin Brothers pottery; Deren Coetzer for bee keeping; Omesh Somaroo, Nikki Moodley, Al Diesel and the Soni family for information on Hindu practice; Sanghamitra Mukherjee for helping to pack Mercy's tiffin tin; the late Mr. Bandhoo from the Pietermaritzburg Gandhi Society and Richard Steel for chatting to me about Ghandi; Joan Kerchhoff for reminiscing about the history of civil disobedience in 'Maritzburg; Robin Crouch for his V&F columns in the Witness archive; Clint Frost for advice on how to jimmy a bobcat; Nico Pascarel for French dialogue; and Andrew Line for imagining the dealings of a devious property developer. Thanks Bethy Meijer for the "loan" of Lemon; and thanks Jenny Kerchhoff, for last-minute proofreading from your hospital bed. Thanks too to Ciaran Hornby for reading a very unpolished manuscript twice. Thank you, Faber Academy and Tom Bromley in particular, for your on-line writing course that helped me to up my game. And so much gratitude to Jessica Powers from Catalyst Press who first agreed to publish this story in the USA and to Isabelle Bleeker and Jennifer Thompson from the Nordlyset Literary Agency for brokering a deal with Walker Books and sending Mercy out into the world to seek her fortune. Thanks too, to Mara Bergman for welcoming me so warmly into the fold at Walker Books.

And finally, to my dear family—Anton, Davie and Simon—as well as Mum, Dad, Fi, Helen and Jamie—thank you for walking this road with me. How did I get so lucky?

Author Bridget Krone

Bridget Krone lives and works in a village called Hilton just outside Pietermaritzburg, in the foothills of the Drakensberg mountains in South Africa. She has spent most of her working life writing short novels and English language text books for school children in South Africa. Her favorite stories are those that, just when you expect a lesson, sing a song instead.

Illustrator Karen Vermeulen

Karen Vermeulen is an illustrator, designer, art director, and writer living in Cape Town, South Africa. She has designed the majority of Catalyst Press's book covers. She works from a corner of her small flat, her desk facing Table Mountain. She loves humor, stories, patterns and color. Her cat (Sir Henry) loves walking over her keyboard and lying on top of her drawings while she tries to work.